To My Best friend

xxx
Barb

CH00431522

At The End Of A Lullaby

Barbara Lloyd Davies

Pen Press Publishers Ltd

First published in Great Britain by
Pen Press Publishers Ltd
39-41, North Road
Islington
London N7 9DP

ISBN 1-904754-31-7

Printed and bound in the UK

A catalogue record of this book is available from the
British Library

Cover design Jacqueline Abromeit

To my husband,
my love, my life.
my inspiration and my strength.

To Hilary and Billy
my most treasured friends.

About the Author

Barbara Lloyd Davies trained as an actress in Liverpool and has worked in all areas of theatre and television. Her career has seen her take on many different roles as both an actor and a writer.

Barbara and co. author Roy Brandon wrote the play "The Little Feller" recently produced by Playhouse Studios, a production Barbara also performed in. She has acted in threatre and panto productions for a variety of theatre companies up and down the country, taking on both comical and serious parts. Research into child sex abuse cases for Social Services involved her playing various children's roles whilst working with trainee social workers.

At The End Of A Lullaby is a novel that encompases many real life aspects of Manchester and Liverpool, areas the author knows particularly well.

Now living in North Wales with her husband, Barbara is very proud of being a Stepmum - a welcome job she successfully combines with her continuing writing and acting career.

At The End
Of A
Lullaby

Part One

CHAPTER ONE

Morgan Lahiff stood at the top of the Minaun cliffs, shielding herself from the wind and rain that lashed at her from all directions. Clutching the bundle tight to her breast, the woman gazed down upon the raging Atlantic below. This was it, there was no place left to run and nowhere to hide. The small drawbridge that connected Achill Island to the mainland had been raised due to the treacherous conditions. Now there was no way of the Island, she was trapped.

The past flashed before her. A childhood spent on Achill had been fun and carefree. Roaming up and down the many cliffs, swimming in the calm Atlantic on hot summer days. Playing out until the hours of darkness told you it was time to go home. What a tomboy she had been, despite her delicate frame and long golden hair, and the intensity of her green eyes, glittering with spirit and vitality. Life on the Island had been so exciting and adventure lurked everywhere on the wide open bog land. To an imaginative young girl, the mountains and cliffs took on all kinds of guises: huge towering monsters one day, and perhaps pyramids the next.

Then came her teenage years, when she no longer cared to run from cliff to cliff and the thought of wet hair prevented her from swimming in the sea she had once so loved. Nothing stayed the same forever; the games she had played as a little girl now seemed childish and held no interest for her. Outside, beyond the land of Achill, there was a big world, a world where anything was possible. Morgan spent many hours poring over the magazines that sat on the shelves of Mrs. O'Malley's local shop, magazines that told of high street fashion, music and dancing, makeup and boys - yes, even them too. This world she longed to be part of, as she planned her escape to the big city.

At sixteen, she had saved enough money to set herself up in Manchester. Willing to take any job that would allow her to pay her rent, Morgan accepted a position as a chambermaid in a large, swanky hotel. The job was good enough for now; maybe she would do some training later, but right now all she longed for was the excitement of city life.

For two years Morgan played and partied, until that fateful day when her life changed forever.

Accompanied by a wicked hangover and with the bitter taste of last night's vodka still lingering on het palate, Morgan struggled into room 104 with her cleaning trolley. It was the housekeeper's day off, so she could get away with a 'make-do', as the girls called it - a quick flick round with a duster and mop. Job done in no time, without the worry of Mrs Davis conducting one of her rigid inspections. Then down to the staff room for a smoke and two paracetamols.

Morgan made a start in the bathroom. Did anyone actually ever use these bidets, she wondered, apart from washing their smalls in them? Whoever occupied this room liked expensive aftershave. The pure silk shirts that hung on coat hangers told their own tale. No sign of any female presence, either: no feminine toiletries or nicknacks.

Now into the bedroom. Its occupier had a problem. He smoked far too much, judging by the overflowing ashtrays. Probably some high flying businessman under stress - though the display of books by the bedside indicated that he did have enough time to read. Morgan noted the authors' names: Dickens, Webster, John Bunyan and *The Complete Works of Shakespeare*. As she picked up the latter and idly leafed through it, Morgan was not to know that she was also about to open the pages of a new life: one that offered all the glamour and privilege of high society - but told nothing of the price that would have to be paid for living such a life..

She discovered that the middle section of the book had

been removed. Inside its deep hole lay small packages of white powder. Holding them up to look more closely, Morgan didn't quite know what to do. Should she put them back and just forget the whole thing? Or go to the manager? Or even the police?

No time! The door burst open and she dropped everything in panic. Looking straight into the eyes of the returning occupier, she froze. With a becoming aura of coolness, the man picked up the small parcels and replaced them inside the book. His voice was gentle, with a velvety tenor that softened his clipped upper-class accent.

'Let me take that. I do like a good read, don't you? I startled you, I'm sorry. Look, let me make you a coffee.' His manner was smooth and calm as began preparing the cups. 'I was just about to have one, so please join me. It's been a hell of a day and I could do with a chat. This damn pharmaceutical conference is such a bore - everybody competing against each other for the miracle cure. Oh yes, there are many secrets in this industry; you've just found one yourself. Oops, must keep it a secret! One lump or two?'

So that's what it's all about, thought Morgan. She might have known; after all, the hotel was always bustling with all kinds of conference meetings. In fact, one was taking place today in the Mahogany Suite.

Placing a steaming coffee cup in her hand, the man gestured for Morgan to sit. She followed his instruction without question, for he had a commanding manner that did not invite argument. He was tall and lean in stature, and his looks reminded Morgan of an aristocratic old Etonian: well-cared-for olive complexion, warm brown eyes, a head of luxuriant blond hair, smooth high forehead. Despite having a small nose and thin lips, he was alarmingly attractive, she decided.

'Conran Blake,' he said, offering her his hand. 'Pleased to meet you.'

'Morgan - Morgan Lahiff.'

'Well Morgan, how long have you worked here?'

She found herself answering all his questions; he seemed so genuinely interested in what she had to say about Manchester and city life. Soon they were talking as if they had known each other for years. By the time she left room 104, she had accepted a date for dinner with the stranger. Still stunned by the speed of events, she began to dwell on what she had found inside the book. Well, he had explained himself and of course it was more than possible. After all, drug dealers didn't stay in big posh hotels, did they? No, they hung around street corners waiting for their prey, mostly youngsters, according to the media. And Conran hadn't shown any alarm on discovering her with the samples; it must be as he said, Morgan was sure: some sort of cure he wanted to keep quiet. How exciting! Perhaps it was a cure for cancer or something equally ground breaking.

That afternoon, she had a disturbed sleep in front of the TV. Her dreams were vivid and disturbing. On waking, she showered and dressed for the evening. Unfortunately, a chambermaid's salary didn't run to Yves St. Laurent, so it was a cheap black dress from the high street and court shoes to match. But Morgan had been blessed with the kind of looks that took no great effort to enhance, so she looked good in whatever she wore. She combed back her long, thick mane of golden hair, then it was a quick pat of makeup, and she was ready. One last look in the mirror at her gentle curves, the elegant length and shape of her legs. Her dove-soft skin glowed with the radiance and freshness of youth, and her deep-set green eyes promised both magnetic sensuality and innocence.

Morgan was a Catholic, and although she enjoyed the excitement of the Manchester club scene, as yet she had stayed 'intact', as her mother (God rest her soul) would have called it. Some things remained with a person from childhood, and her virginity had been one of those things for Morgan, who had never broken completely free of the many Catholic traditions ingrained in her as a child. Though her parents had loved life and enjoyed the local dances, claiming it was fine to have a good time and enjoy the many pleasures the good lord had bestowed upon them, boys and sex were always discouraged for their daughter. Pre-marital sex would remain a sin on Achill forever, or so it seemed. Her father, when he was alive, had watched over her like a hawk whenever they attended the local barn dances. His old-fashioned way had been funny to her then. Morgan wondered now what her mother and father would have thought of her going out with a complete stranger. Was he even a good catholic boy? Somehow she thought not!

A car horn aroused her from her daydream. Morgan closed the door on her shabby bedsit, not knowing that she was closing the door on innocence and freedom.

A British racing green Jensen Interceptor stood like a monster outside the building that made up the five individual tenements the landlord liked to call bedsits. Conran Blake instantly knew that this girl wouldn't give him too much trouble. He had to admit that she did have something that separated her from the rest of the beautiful mistresses he'd loved and left. He couldn't quite put a finger on it, but she was interesting. He'd taken a chance on her already. After all, she hadn't squealed to the hotel or the police, had she? Surely she must have known what the packages were? This was Manchester, for God's sake! Yet he'd done a pretty good job of charming her. Well, not many women could refuse his advances. She had been forthcoming in the hotel room and he quite liked the quaint lilt of her Irish accent, it had amused him. No, this girl would be fun and something a little different. Why hadn't he noticed her before? He owned the hotel, after all. Blake made a mental note to pay more attention in the future.

His hotel was proving as lucrative as his casino. Billing Casino was his first love and plans for other additions to Blake Enterprises included more casinos to be opened down south. Conran was not alone in his love of the good life and obtaining a gambling licence year after year had proved easy, thanks to the local Chief of Police, who also enjoyed life in the fast lane. It was this association that allowed Blake to participate with ease in his other little ventures, such as drug-running.

Conran had started out small-time with a bit of blow for himself and his college pals. Then it was onto amphetamines, from where he had quickly progressed to coke. His own personal use had stopped after college. Everyone knew drugs were a mug's game unless you were the supplier. He looked on himself as a businessman simply supplying a need, with the profits outweighing the risks.

The packages Morgan had found were samples from a new supplier. Generally he didn't handle the stuff - that's what he paid staff for, but each new assignment had to be checked, and that he always did himself. No, he'd soon have Miss Lahiff eating out of the palm of his hand. How long would it be before he got bored with her? Hard to tell - but, one way or another, women were never a problem to get rid of.

Morgan sat in the passenger seat, feeling quite the lady and doing a very good job of stopping her knees from knocking. Intimidated by the sheer luxury of the car, she felt stupid. After eighteen years of being a poor Catholic girl, sixteen of them spent listening to sermons of hell and damnation, how could a car possibly intimidate her? No, she must pull herself together and act as sophisticated as she looked.

They sped off at a furious pace, Conran apologising for driving so fast. Morgan assured him she didn't mind; she enjoyed watching the fields flash by the windows. The countryside reminded her of home. Conran kept casting sidelong glances at the girl, taken aback, in spite of himself, by her beauty. He was looking forward to the evening ahead.

The drive was long and Morgan grew edgy. After all, she didn't know this guy; he could be a mass murderer for all she knew. She'd heard all sorts of things in the news, women and girls murdered, bodies found in woods, stuff like that. Oh God! What was she thinking of? Too late now, she couldn't go back.

Conran sensed her unease. It made him laugh. What had he caught in his net this time, he wondered.

Dinner was at Renoirs, an intimate lakeside restaurant just outside Manchester. It was a particular favourite of Conran's, probably because the chef was one of his best clients. If you cared to look, it was surprising who enjoyed the odd shot of coke. Sure, the world would tell you to look on the streets for your average junkie. Bullshit! Everyone took drugs of some sort, whether it was alcohol, speed or coke. Everyone had a favourite drug, and Conran supplied the best, cleanest cut gear, so he was Mr Popular. Didn't he often give away freebies to his friends and clients when they were a little short of cash? A deal here, a loan there, his generosity never failing to make him useful contacts. Yet he ran a tight outfit. He had the best and the most loyal members of the Mancunian underworld at his feet.

Once they were seated, the menu was delivered with the customary grace of the Maitre d.

'Sorry, my dear there doesn't seem to be any Irish stew on the Menu', he laughed.

Completely ignoring this comment, Morgan looked into the eyes of the Maitre d, smiled and delivered her choice in perfect French. Surpassing herself she continued to choose from the wine menu after much deliberation between herself and the Maitre d, who by this time was almost convinced he was in love.

Such a beauty and so young, such taste and eloquence. It was obvious to him that this young lady could hold her own in the best of French restaurants. Conran, too, seemed impressed, so Morgan decided not to tell him about Uncle William's famous restaurant on Achill, nor about the excitement of meeting all the French chefs who had visited the restaurant every summer. In fact she decided not to mention Achill at all. No, if he asked, she would tell him she was from Dublin. That would make her look more worldly, more experienced.

'Well, I am impressed,' Conran murmured, smiling at her.

Morgan smiled back coyly. 'What did you expect? Never underestimate the Irish, Mr. Blake.'

How charming he thought her, and obviously a little fiery. He liked that. It made a nice change from the usual dim and doll-like creatures he had become accustomed to entertaining. They spent the rest of the meal making polite chitchat whilst being serenaded by the sounds of Nat King Cole. The setting was perfect, the music likewise, and the meal was a gourmet's delight.

Was it the setting or perhaps just the wine that made Morgan feel she was falling in love for the first time? She had almost forgotten that she knew nothing about this guy - everything just felt so natural, so familiar. Conran had said he was in finance, on business with his company holding their yearly conference in the hotel. His company, he said, provided funding for many things, research into groundbreaking pharmaceutical products being just one. Should she ask what those packages contained? No, she didn't want to spoil things by appearing too nosy. After a long run of uninspiring boyfriends her own age, here at last was a man she felt deeply mentally and physically attracted to. His conversation was stimulating, his voice compelling and his style charmingly individual. By comparison, boys her own age seemed insipid and shallow. Was she was mentally older than her eighteen years? Who cared? Conran was new and exciting and that was all that mattered.

Back in the car, Morgan fastened her seatbelt and began to relax, looking forward to the rest of the evening, which was far from over. From Renoirs they descended on Billings Casino, which was obviously the place to be seen. The off-the-shoulder evening gowns worn by the female croupiers, influenced by the classical Greek and Roman style, made them all look like film stars. The male croupiers were equally sophisticated in red trousers with black cummerbunds and crisp white shirts. Everything about the casino was opulent. The thick red carpet, the mahogany tables edged with gold trimmings looked lavish and antique. When Morgan looked up to the ceiling, a collage not unlike Michaelangelo's in the Sistine Chapel stared back down at her. Never had she seen such a place.

At table after table, her host lost money. But he didn't seem to mind. Hell, that must have been a week's salary he had just thrown away, Morgan mused. Was he trying to be flash? Well, that was his prerogative on the first date. She tried hard not to look too impressed.

The drive home seemed only to take minutes. Conran pulled to a halt outside Morgan's bedsit, and she invited him in for coffee. Hardly giving her the opportunity to put the kettle on, he was upon her, covering her with long, lingering kisses that aroused instincts she found hard to resist. Holding her firmly, his hands reached for the long blonde hair that cascaded down her back like a golden waterfall. Gripping it tightly, he pressed his body into hers. How desperately she wanted him, how good it would have been to give in. Her loins ached with a desire she had never known before, yet the good Catholic girl in her got a grip. Pulling away, she held her breath. He sensed her fear and loosened his grip, gently releasing her.

'I'm sorry really, I never meant to... I don't know what came over me. I'll go. God, I didn't mean to give you the wrong impression.' He turned to the door.

'No, really, it's just that it's late and I'm on duty early tomorrow.'

'Of course. Look, why don't you stop by my room tomorrow. It's the last day of the conference. We could have a coffee, perhaps?'

She agreed to visit him the next morning, halfway through her shift. Damn! That would mean she would have to get up extra early to wash her hair and make sure she looked her best.

Later, as she lay in bed, questions flooded her consciousness. Questions that she didn't have answers to. Why her? He was so handsome and rich, why had he chosen her?

As he drove away Conran Blake made a mental note to have Miss Morgan Lahiff fired the very next day. First he would make her needy and vulnerable; he intended to play with her for a while. Tonight had been fun and he would like a little more fun. So he would set himself up as a knight in shining armour. He had a plan.

Rather than going straight back to the hotel, Conran went to The Readings Room, one of Manchester's oldest drinking establishments, which still barred women, except in special circumstances. He had his own quarters there, from which he conducted much of his business.

Inside the bar, he was greeted by his right-hand man, Gregory Scott. Scott was not a popular man in the area; he was not known for his sense of humour or good will. In fact, he was exactly the kind of man Blake liked to have close to him. Towering above most people, he was a man of few words and many deeds - destructive deeds.

Gregory Scott seemed to live solely for Blake, who had first found him performing as a doorman for clubs in the heart of Skimsdale, a notoriously rough area of the city, known locally as 'the concrete jungle'. The new town was an area that mainly consisted of over-spill from nearby Liverpool. Blake had got wind of Scott, a heavy who held several doors in the town. He had set various tests to see if the man could be taken, sending one or two of his best men to see if he could outrun the guy and take his patch. It was all to no avail. So this was the guy for Conran Blake.

Of course he had many others on his payroll. At least two hundred doormen countrywide, who doubled as drug dealers, hit-men, arms dealers and go-betweens. Blake Enterprises also had a female section based at the casino. Most of the girls worked as croupiers. The ones who knew the score were loyal, discreet and mostly too afraid to speak out of turn. Blake remained anonymous to the others, who were just casual employees taking instructions from their manager.

And that was the way Conran Blake liked it.

CHAPTER TWO

'Any calls?'

'No, it's been quiet tonight.'

'Okay, next on my list of things to do? Ah yes Linda's exit interview.'

Conran was fully aware that Linda's cold turkey period was over, and the girl would be back to full health.

'Yes, sir.'

Dumb bitch! A couple of fucks and the girl was under the impression that she had a monopoly on him. Typical woman! Once rejected they go straight to the coppers and tell the lot. How very amusing! If only she had known that he had watched her every move. Did she really think security was so lacking? Oh Linda, Linda! How quickly she had tied the noose around her own neck. The little girl had been given a chance to be good, to put the whole thing down to a good time and go back to the casino and work for him, which was all she'd ever been doing, in his opinion. Ah well, *que sera sera*. That's the way the cookie crumbled.

Linda hadn't gone to work now for over a month on advice from the police, who had assured her that she had done the right thing in exposing this criminal. Her duty to society was truly fulfilled. Little did she know that not two minutes after she had left the police station, CID Officer Brian Reynolds had made a hasty phone call to Conran Blake's office.

Linda's flat was cold, where once it had been warm and cosy, thanks to Conran and the job he gave her, not to mention the extras he provided - free crack and dope in generous amounts. Oh, but that had been when he desired her. Anything she had wanted was hers, all in a space of three months, from the date of her employment as a croupier at Billing Casino. Now she was alone with her fear and very little of anything else. Why hadn't the police offered her protection? Why hadn't they called her back for questioning over the affairs of one Mr Conran Blake? Still, they had said these things take time.

She shivered and pulled the quilt tighter around her. The flash apartment Conran had promised her had never materialised. Just loose promises once again. Damp seeped into the walls of the council flat, causing the cheap wallpaper to hang loose from the walls and the ceiling. The linoleum covered by a small hearthrug stank of damp and decay. The bedroom was now unfit for habitation, since winter had come and she could no longer afford to heat the place as she once had. Ice froze to the inside of the windows, almost causing them to crack. Maybe things would be easier once her social came through. How long could she go on living like this? Hungry and cold almost too scared to walk the street in broad daylight, let alone nightfall. Something told her that he knew, that he was laughing, possibly even watching her and gloating at the suffering she endured.

That was ridiculous. Was she paranoid? She told the manager that she needed time off work to go home to Liverpool, to nurse her sick mother. No-one could know that she had no family - or so she naively thought. And even if he didn't believe her, Conran would have thought that she was simply nursing her wounded pride. Well, he was wrong. She didn't like being used and thrown away like some toy left over from Christmas. It had been a one-way direct walk to the police. Conran Blake had it coming.

She'd done her stint of cold turkey, 'Hell on God's living earth' she called it. Her counsellor had said that she was on the mend and not to rush things. Maybe once the police got some hard evidence, they could bring him in. Then she would be free. Meanwhile, she endured a harsh living on what little cash she had.

The phone startled her. Linda slipped her hand free from the warmth and comfort of the blanket. Shaking, she held onto the receiver, showing a weakness that was not at all healthy.

'Linda, it's me, Wendy. Look, sorry I haven't been round. It's bloody mayhem at the casino, we're so short staffed. I've just finished my shift. Look, give me twenty minutes. I'm coming round. I'll bring us a bottle or two. How does that sound?'

'Thank God. I'm going crazy here on my own. Can you pick me up a packet of fags on your way round? I can't wait to see you. Hurry up!'

Linda replaced the receiver. Maybe things would get better after all. It was nice of Wendy to call just when she thought she had no friends. Things could just be looking up.

In Conran Blake's office Wendy replaced the receiver.

'Well done, now be a good girl and run along, you'll find the rewards of your work in your salary.'

Wendy left. Having worked for the outfit for over four years, she knew better than to ask questions, let alone refuse Mr Blake's orders. After all, wasn't it every girl for herself?

Linda started to have a tidy around. Despite the cold, she changed into something a little more cheerful, not wanting to depress Wendy, who seemed the nearest thing she had to a best friend right now. She put on more makeup to hide the ravages of cold turkey and poverty. Her body didn't look too bad, and the cloud of dark curly hair still gave her that sultry look. She had the kind of looks that immediately turned men into helpless little boys. All men, that is, except Conran Blake.

Once all this was over she was gonna take a real job, maybe even retrain. One day she would get married and have children, own her own house with some loving husband who would be kind to her. Then maybe she'd even try to find out who her real mother was. She had a future, that was the main thing, and now she even had a friend.

Ah, there was Wendy now. Linda rushed to the front door, happily anticipating some female company. Removing all the chains and safety catches, she pulled open the door with a heart which was just that little bit lighter.

By the time she arrived in his office, Linda's colour was whiter than white. This is where it had all started for her. The rustling sound of the Chesterfield suite had echoed her own moans of pleasure as Conran Blake had brought her to heights of intense passion, thrusting into her deeply, forcefully. How many nights had he taken her in this very room, before her shift started? They had shared a lust that Linda had foolishly mistaken for love. Now she realised that she had simply been dancing with the devil.

Like a stranded swan, she stood before him now, a pitiful creature consumed by fear. Sitting behind his desk, power oozed from him. He looked in control, in charge - as indeed he was. Four over-sized monkeys had assembled for the entertainment. Gregory Scott was not one of them, because he did not have the type of needs a woman could fulfil. No, despite his outward machismo, he liked his meat young, sweet and male. Most of the croupiers had left except for a rather cherubic-looking boy whom Blake had hired expressly for the pleasure of Gregory Scott.

'How kind of you to join us this evening, Linda, my lovely.'

'Conran, please, what's going on?'

'Allow me to introduce you to a friend of mine, although I think you two are already acquainted.'

Brian Reynolds, head of the CID, made his entrance like some ring-master at a circus of horrors, and top of the bill for entertainment was Linda Thomas. She began to shake violently.

She began to plead. 'Please, Conran, I... Oh, God help me!'

Removing his belt, Conran gave a little laugh of pure masochistic delight. She felt the first sting as it brought her to her knees, blood rushing from the cut made by the silver buckle.

'Pick her up!' ordered the boss. Two men did so, holding up the helpless body for further abuse. Letting her come round a little, Conran spoke gently, softly, like a father to a child.

'Did you betray me?'

She didn't answer.

'Did you betray me, my darling?'

'Conran, please! Let me go. I won't say anything, not this time. I swear!'

He started to sing a lullaby, just like his mother used to do, before she beat the living daylights out of him. For his mother, it had been the only way to teach.

'*Hush little baby, don't say a word, Poppa's going to buy you a mocking bird; and if that mocking bird don't sing, poppa's going to buy you a diamond ring.*'

The melody ended as Blake, now in full flight, tore the clothes off her back. She tried to shield herself and hide her nakedness from the men in the room. She searched for help and pity in their eyes, but there was none. They dared not look away or show any kind of weakness. No, a grass was grass. A sinner needed to be punished and dealt with, it went without saying. The fate of the informer was never a tasteful one. The pain took Linda's breath away as the second lash tore into her fragile flesh.

'The desk!' Conran was almost in a frenzy, the adrenaline rising inside him, power dousing his brain like a drug. 'The desk! Hold her face down!'

The men obeyed, looking scared themselves.

'Mr Reynolds, you should have the first pleasure. Let's just say it's my gift to you. After all, it's only right and fitting.'

This was a test; the CID man must show no pity. There was never any room for pity in this life of deceit he had carved for himself. One day, if he was not careful, he too would pay a price. But for now, he would protect his own, and that meant his wife and children. Fuck it, she was just some dried up slag anyway. Grabbing the torrent of black hair that now held traces of blood, Reynolds rammed his self-hatred and loathing forcibly into the pathetic body.

Linda's cries were in vain as each man took his pleasure with her, goaded by her ex-lover, Conran Blake, who watched with interest. When the last was done she fell to the floor. Conran took the pistol out of the top drawer of his desk. Nobody tried to stop him.

Leaning close to her, he murmured: 'Do you love me? I want to hear you say it. Do you love me?'

'Yes, I love you,' she breathed.

'Then you know what to do,'

He handed her the pistol. She took it almost with gratitude. Linda Thomas blew a hole in the side of her head. Her body was never recovered, and nobody ever asked about her.

Morgan was looking forward to meeting her new Mr Swaree; her mood was good today. She felt sort of prosperous, though couldn't quite understand why. Things were definitely on the up.

It was much colder than usual for the time of year. Winter normally delayed its true onslaught until January. Still, the early morning frost gave Manchester's inner city a crisp, glacial freshness. Soon it would be time to start putting up the Christmas tree in the foyer of the hotel. That was a job Morgan liked. Christmas at the hotel was fun, not like home perhaps, but then, since the death of her mother, Christmas had never been the same.

What celebrations they'd had once the dreaded church service was over! Family and friends joined together to honour Christ's birth, packed tightly into Achill's tiny, run-down chapel. The service seemed to take hours, or was it the fact that it was always cold in there? Even in summer, the church had been cold and draughty. Father Mural would preach for hours in his monotonous drawl that almost sent you to sleep. But then after mass, everyone gathered to take a small glass of something on this special day.

Mother always cooked a goose - usually one that had last been seen running around the garden, happily unaware of its imminent fate. Father would build a strong fire, guaranteed to warm away the chilblains collected in church. Presents would be unwrapped after dinner - simple but pleasing gifts - then, dressed for the extremely cold climate, the family would walk the long deserted road, calling in on neighbours to share good tidings. On the journey home Father would be quite tipsy, thanks to all the mulled wine, not to mention the odd glass of poteen nobody was supposed to know about. Christmas evening would be spent playing charades and finally listening to tales of old Ireland, related in a mesmerising voice by father, who loved an audience.

Those days were gone now. Only Uncle Robert was left in the great stone farmhouse, though he was happy enough, for he was a quiet man who liked his own company. He would have Christmas lunch with friends and then fall asleep in front of the TV. There was nothing for Morgan to travel home for.

Running into the locker room, she came to a halt at the sign on her locker door: 'PLEASE COME TO MY OFFICE IMMEDIATELY.MRS DAVIS.'

Shit! Was it possible that Mrs Davis had found out about her date with Conran? The hotel did not like staff to indulge in any sort of familiarity with the patrons. No, she'd been discreet. Then what? No use speculating. Only one way to find out.

'Morgan, please come in.'

A memo had been delivered that very morning from the manager Jerry Hughes, announcing that cutbacks were necessary if the hotel was to have a future. Therefore each section had to reduce its staff numbers. This was bad news for Kathy Davis, who had been under the impression that business was good. After all, weren't they fully booked for Christmas? Letting her favourite member of staff go was not a task she relished, but Morgan had been the last full-time member of staff to join Mrs Davis's section, so she had no other option. Still, Morgan was young and intelligent. Hadn't Mrs. Davis always said that the girl was wasted as a chambermaid?

'Morgan, I'm afraid I have bad news. There's only one way I can say this, and that's to get straight to the point. We have to let you go at the end of the week. There'll be a month's salary waiting for you. I'm sorry, my love, really, but there's nothing I can do about it, I'm afraid.'

Morgan was bewildered. 'I... er, I don't know what to say. It's all a bit of a shock. I...' Her voice trailed off.

'I'm so sorry, my dear.'

What was she to do now? Christmas alone in the bedsit? No companionship or hustle and bustle at the hotel to see her through the festive season - and no cash. Perhaps she should go home, but what the hell for? Going home for a well-deserved holiday was one thing, going home in despair was another.

'Well, I'd better get on while I still have a job,' she said, moving towards the door.

Damn Conran Blake, thought Mrs Davis as she watched the young woman leave.

Approaching room 104, Morgan paused. Should she knock, or just leave things for now? After all, she had decisions to make - one of them being whether to start looking for a job in the same field, or to try something different. It was a well-known fact that Manchester was going through an employment crisis, so it wouldn't be easy.

Her hand rapped on the door almost before she had realised what she had done.

'It's open, come in.'

'Hi, you did say to pop in.'

'That's right,' smiled Conran. 'Hey, you look a little peaky this morning. Come and sit down. Let's get you a hot drink.'

'I came to thank you for last night.'

Today found Conran dressed in a polo shirt, a blue jumper and jeans. Morgan liked the way he looked in his casual wear: sort of broad with a pert little butt and small waist. His blonde hair fell over the front of his eyes as he went to plug in the kettle. Sweeping it out of his face, he turned to face her with all the sincerity of an archbishop. This guy was good, very good!

It was something in his brown eyes that brought the first tear trickling down her cheek. Their expression warmed and comforted her soul.

'Hey, hey what's this?' he crooned. Like a concerned parent, he reached for her and held her protectively for a while, humming a tune softly into her hair.

'What's that you're humming?' she asked.

'Just a little song my mother sang to me, to soothe me and calm me down if I got angry or just sad.'

Morgan felt a total fool. She'd never been one for crying; crying never solved anything.

'Sorry to be such a baby. It's just that I…er… I got fired today.' Relaying the story of her interview with Mrs. Davis brought about more tears.

'Look, I don't know if you'll be interested, or maybe I'm interfering, but I have a friend who's desperate for staff at his casino. I could put in a word for you if you like.'

'No, really, it's not your problem.'

'Well, okay, but you'd be doing me a favour, you know. I owe this guy, so it would be my pay back to him.'

Morgan Lahiff took to the casino like a duck to water. The customers grew fond of her, as did the staff. Everyone except the special employees of Conran Blake loved her. To the people who belonged to Blake's underworld she was nothing more than another tart, heading down the road to destruction. Of course nobody ever told her what had happened to the girl who had previously worked table nine, the blackjack table. When somebody went missing you didn't sing the song around. You kept your mouth shut, and asked no questions, unless you fancied a journey down the same track. No, they could do nothing except let this seemingly naïve little Irish girl walk into the trap so many others had fallen into.

At the end of every shift Conran would be sure to meet her. She was never aware that while she was working, he'd been looking down on her through the internal security monitors situated on the top floor of the casino.

Conran wondered how long little Morgan would work table nine. For there was something about that particular table…

CHAPTER THREE

Each night he would leave by the back staircase. The car would be brought round and he would then drive it to the front and escort her out.

Morgan had a passion for life. In the two weeks before Christmas, Conran Blake took her wining and dining. They made a short trip to London to watch the best of the West End shows, and afterwards discussed the performances with a passion. Her hunger to see and visit everything touched him. The Tower of London was her particular favourite, so much history, 'spicy history', she called it. Henry the Eighth, what a guy! A monster! Did people like that really exist? Poor Ann Boleyn had been beheaded, and Morgan had shed a tear for the hapless queen as if she'd known her personally. Blake had found that so touching.

Conran would combine these trips with his various business dealings. He'd simply tell Morgan that he had a meeting with some finance company or other, being careful never to give her any additional information. Occasionally she asked about his work and the endless meetings he had to attend; he simply muttered something about fluctuations in the Stock Market and their impact on his financial dealings. He made it sound uninteresting, and she remained in the dark regarding his true enterprise.

In spite of himself, Conran was growing fonder of her by the day. He hated to admit it, but the emotions inside him were stronger than anything he had ever felt before. This came as a shock to him, for previously, admiration of physical beauty was the nearest he had ever got to love. This time he felt possessive, even jealous, of Morgan's gift for living and loving, for seeing the good in all. Yes, he was even jealous of her innocence! Could he possibly be in love with Morgan Lahiff?

To her, he was everything she could ever have wished for. Patient, charming, kind and thoughtful. Hadn't he shown her the greatest of respect? He'd never pushed his advances on her. Goodnight kisses (albeit deeply passionate ones) were all he had asked. They had separate rooms in hotels; no stay-overs at his or her place. To Morgan, theirs was exactly the kind of pure and wholesome relationship she needed.

Over the past month, Conran Blake had been the perfect gent. But when the door closed on Morgan, a woman would be sent to him to satisfy his needs.

Hilary, who took care of the female staff at the casino, was a firm favourite with him. She was experienced and in the know about his real business, having worked for the outfit for the past five years. She had never married, had never really thought about it. Her only child spent most of her time with a baby-sitter, as Hilary was seldom around, and showed little interest in the girl. Pregnancy was something she had not planned and she'd only discovered her condition when she was already six months pregnant. Still, what the hell, who gave a fuck? There were always child minders and nurseries.

Hilary knew Conran and what he liked, and boy did she give it to him. Her looks were hard, streetwise, the type of looks a woman has when she's been around the block a few times. Perhaps she was a little rough around the edges, she had one too many grey hairs, but she still showed flashes of youth, which, mingled with experience, gave her that special something. Her dark, smoky features still commanded the attention of many a man. And when Hilary laughed, she was so charismatic, one couldn't help being charmed.

Yet the blackness of her eyes could have come from the devil himself. She had a very dark side to her. Her temper was explosive, and her physical ability to fight hand to hand was something many a man and woman had experienced to their detriment. And there was one group of people for whom she reserved a near-pathological - and, to her, utterly justified - hatred: the Irish...

Somehow, being with this woman made Conran remember his mother. Her short, greying hair brought him strange comfort. There was no more comforting feeling than being held close to a firm, large, motherly bosom.

Hilary adored and respected Conran for who he was, and the organisation he headed. She aimed to stay at the top of the Blake empire, to hold on to the respect her position had brought her. She had started her own outfit by the time she was twenty-seven, and knew every trick in the book. There was not a scam Hilary couldn't or hadn't pulled, be it cheque fraud or counterfeiting. She enjoyed her work. On meeting Conran Blake, she had recognised an opportunity to progress into a bigger league, and she intended to please him in all things. She was independent and liked it that way. While paying the bills had once been a struggle, now she could buy what she wanted, when she wanted.

Yet, behind the respectable veneer of a job and financial security, Hilary hid a deeply disturbed past. She had never been young or carefree; her childhood and teenage years had been spent in a state of emotional turmoil, flitting from one gang to another, from the intrusive fingering of a sexually depraved father to the arms of her first lover, who had doubled as her pimp.

But not for long. Hilary learned fast and soon became capable of taking care of herself - in whatever way necessary.

CHAPTER FOUR

When Conran Blake walked through the door of his mansion, his favourite mongrel, Timmy, bounded up to meet him. He stroked the animal lovingly, thinking: if only people could be as trustworthy as dogs. Mrs Atkinson, his housekeeper, had left a warm fire in the hearth, along with a bottle of his best port. As the port hit the back of his throat, Conran felt a stirring in his loins. How he longed to show his Irish rose what he was capable of! He imagined undressing her, introducing his tongue to her most intimate female parts, inserting his manhood into that delicate frame. He phoned the casino and asked for Hilary to come over, then began to pace round the huge house.

It consisted of three storeys but, although it was tall, its height was deceptive, for the turns and passageways of the house were narrow and confined. The decor was reminiscent of the Victorian period, although some modernisation had been carried out over the many years Conran had lived there, mainly in the kitchen and living room. The house still contained the old library, full of unread and dusty volumes, and an oak desk added to its air of learning. Rooms at the top of the house were rarely used; most contained his mother's modest collection of clothes. The rooms on the middle floor could have been mistaken for any well-furnished Sixties' apartment. Below, in the bowels of the house, were a cellar, and next to that a small room, barely noticeable because its door blended into the wall. It appeared to be a room of no particular importance or interest. Or was it just supposed to look that way?

For this was no ordinary room. One wall was studded with hooks and manacles. Long-tentacled whips dripped from the ceiling. Leather outfits hung, incongruously neat, from a metal rail. A cage, suspended from the ceiling, dominated the room, and machetes adorned the other walls, together with historical armoury of all kinds. The atmosphere was tarnished with the smells of lust and sin; the walls stank of sweat and condensation.

Years earlier, in this same room, young Eileen Blake had given birth to her son, the agonized cries of childbirth muffled and unheard in the depths of the house. The child she bore was a child of sin, and did not deserve to be treated as other children. No, in this room the Blakes hid the shame of their daughter's wanton behaviour.

Now, the scene of his uncelebrated birth was the room where Conran enacted his darkest pleasures. Not everyone entering it did so willingly.

On this occasion, however, both parties were delighted to be there. A fire had been lit in the big hearth and several lanterns gave off a soft if rather eerie glow.

'Mummy, have I been bad?' pleaded a voice.

'Oh, my darling,' said the woman dressed in black, holding a ferocious looking leather strap. 'You have been so bad that mummy must make you better and show you how bad your deeds are. Now my child, prepare yourself.'

With complete abandon, Conran Blake fell on all fours, exposing his naked buttocks. The strap slashed across him three times, leaving red swelling welts on his flesh..

'I'm sorry, Mummy. I won't be bad again, ever. I promise.'

'Crawl to Mummy. Come along, darling, mummy's here to comfort you after your punishment'

Oh so slowly, the boy-man crawled on his hands and knees to his 'mother'. Searching, his mouth found the hard and comforting nipple, sucking on it, nibbling like the child he had once been, brought to safety and a longing for his real mother. Laying him down, Hilary rubbed her hand along his fine long legs, eventually seeking his penis and rubbing the skin up and down.

'There, there now, is that better? Is that what you wanted, you naughty boy? Oh, now, how hard are you getting, my little love? No, no be sure not to spurt that bad thing at Mummy now, or she will have to make you sore again.'

Hilary knew exactly what to do. Two years earlier, she had tuned into what her master needed. It hadn't taken much figuring out, not when she'd done it professionally so many times before.

It was necessary therapy for Conran Blake. For those in control often need the release of being controlled.

Still wrapped up in a blanket, Morgan ran to open the front door. God, it was freezing! Surely there would be a white Christmas this year. Did it have to be so bloody cold though?

'Conran, I wasn't expecting you!'

'Come on, lazy, get up, get dressed, get packed.'

'What?'

'Christmas in Scotland. How does that sound? You didn't have any other plans, did you?'

'Well no, but what about my job? I can't just let the casino down like that. They've been really good to me.'

'Sorted.'

Morgan wasn't sure if she liked this. He had no right interfering with her work. Yes, he'd got her the job, and she would be eternally grateful, but…

'I spoke to my old pal, Warren, and he said it's okay. They can cover for you.'

Morgan's lips were pursed. 'Conran, I'm grateful, but look, you should have consulted me first.'

He had expected her to be overjoyed. Instead she was acting like some spoilt bitch of a child. The bile rose to the top of his throat, a pain flashed across his forehead - the pain he often got when he was angry.

'Right, you don't want to go. I'll cancel the cottage, no bloody problem,' he growled through gritted teeth. Hum the lullaby, he thought, quick, hum the song. That never failed to calm him.

Morgan softened. 'You're singing. You told me you only ever sang or hummed a lullaby when you're upset, or disturbed, or angry. I'm sorry, darling. I didn't mean to be ungrateful. I just... Oh, darling; of course the trip isn't off! It's just that I'm used to my independence, and... Oh, never mind. Come on, you make the coffee, I'll pack the hot water bottles. I think we're gonna need them somehow!'

The journey was long but in such exquisite company how could she fail to be happy? The Scottish scenery was soul embracing. It reminded her of home. Like Achill, the land was vast and rugged. Mountains swirled to form peaks topped with mist like icing on a Christmas cake. The rivers and lakes, now frozen by the frost, added a sparkle to the land, and the trees swayed with the fall of the last drops of snow. This was truly an enchanted place, perhaps a fairytale, and she was the princess with her prince. The world was white and made of ice, and only she and her prince lived on earth to enjoy the seclusion together. No mortal eyes could look at them, or intrude upon their love. As they drove along, she thought of the day she would take Conran to Achill. Perhaps even their children...

'You look deep in thought,' he commented.

'Oh, just thinking, isn't it beautiful? I don't think I'll ever want to go back to Manchester.'

'You will. One week of solitary with me and I'm sure you'll be flagging down the nearest donkey for a lift.'

She hadn't told him about Achill, and where she really came from. No, now wasn't a good time. Not that she'd really needed to lie - but best not to rock the boat. Everything at present was perfect and she was going to make sure it stayed that way.

Crunching along a narrow drive that seemed to go on and on, they eventually came to a small cottage hidden amongst the snow-covered firs. It was dark, but the smell and feel of the crisp air told her everything was perfect for a winter holiday. Dashing out of the car like a child, she ran to the front door of the cottage.

'Hold on! I've got the key.'

'Hurry, hurry, I want to get inside! Come on, slow coach.'

Yes, Conran really cherished this new toy of his. How alive she was, how full of the pleasures of childhood - the pleasures he himself had never known.

Christmas, as most people knew it, hadn't existed for the Blake family. No, it was a sinful waste of time and money. The Lord had expected his sheep to pray and repent of their sins on this special day, not overindulge with greed and selfishness. No, Christmas was a time for prayer. Not that money had been a problem in the huge household his mother kept, and Eileen Blake had adored her only son, adored him with an unhealthy possessiveness. She had felt it her duty to show him the pain that life could bring should he tread a sinful path. At all costs, her son must grow to fear God.

CHAPTER FIVE

Once, Eileen Blake had been beautiful and carefree. Her face seemed to bloom with an innocence even time could not dispel. She was like a porcelain doll, an oh-so-delicate doll that had been given the finest blue eyes, the reddest lips, and the purest white skin. Golden ringlets fought to find space on her shoulders.

So how could this wicked world allow such innocence to be molested, especially by a common village no-good?

At the age of sixteen, Eileen had fallen in love with one of the local boys. Bowled over by his masculinity, flattered by his attention, she had not resisted as Sam Blackthorn laid siege to her. Sam was notorious in the area, having already fathered three children that were known about. But this bit of posh stuff had been a real challenge, so unlike the village girls, who were only too willing to show him a good time for nothing more than a swig of beer. With this bit of well-to-do, Sam felt he had really achieved something. Yet in the end, she had been as easy as the rest, if not easier. It had been nice touching that soft, well cared for complexion, so unlike the rough skin of the village girls. Her hair was clean and you could run your fingers right through it. Every tooth was white, and the taste of her breath had been like ripened apples, sweet and clean.

Eileen received little love at home. In a well-to-do family, it was not unusual that a child should be shown so little attention: children were to be seen and not heard. Mothers did not bring their children up; nannies did. Eileen basked in Sam's insincere affection, revelled in the belief that his kisses meant so much. And when he began to touch her in private places, and said it was because he loved her, she did not doubt him. When his searching fingers had found what lay underneath her petticoat, she had not resisted him, for she wanted so badly to be loved. Sam gave her all that with his touch. He had said they would marry, just as soon as he came into the money he would one day inherit from a rich uncle in Leeds. All this made it okay for Sam to push his thing into her, even though she did not really care for it much. In fact it hurt, and she had bled afterwards. Worried about the thing she had done, Eileen turned to Sam for reassurance. But he had laughed and gone off to drink some ale with his own kind, already bored with his little rich girl.

Of course her well-to-do family had not known of the liaison until the baby started to show. Eileen had been mad to think that her parents would understand, and that she would become the wife of Sam Blackthorn. Eileen's mother was the very pillar of the community, involved in much charity work, while her father held a strong position in local politics and government. Neither could not afford to be tarnished in the public eye.

Sam Blackthorn had been found and asked to leave the area, helped along by two hundred pounds of Mr Blake's money. As for Eileen, there were places a girl could go to be rid of the inconvenient problem of pregnancy, her mother told her. Eileen froze at the thought of losing the child that was growing within her, and refused.

Holding on to the last bit of Sam, and the love she still believed they had shared, Eileen Blake, at the age of seventeen, gave birth to her son in a room situated in the bowels of her family's house. It was a dark, dirty room that was never used. A bed had been placed in there for the very purpose of expurgating her body of the shame it carried. No real care had been taken to cleanse the place, for everyone secretly hoped the child would not survive - everyone except Eileen. All the servants had been paid for their silence and discretion. Any one daring to breathe a word would be dismissed without pay or reference.

The birth had been difficult, bloody and very painful. Eileen's small frame had almost been torn apart by the life that demanded to come forth. It was as well that the act took place in the depths of the house, so none could hear the screams of the child giving birth, joined by those of the child that emerged from her loins.

From that day, Eileen's parents had borne the shame of their immoral daughter. No man would show any interest in the girl now. So the young Eileen was sent away to be educated at a special school, Our Lord of Forgiveness College for Girls, a strict and puritanical Protestant institution. During that time, her baby son saw no light, living only in the basement room of his birth, cared for by the servants.

For three years Eileen was taught to repent her sins of the flesh, and endured the unendurable: the wide cold corridors, the continual prayers, physical punishment in front of the assembled school, malnutrition to the point of near starvation. Indeed many young girls did die there. Who was going to complain about the inhumane conditions? Parents, racked by the shame of their daughters' bastards, would not cry to the authorities and draw further attention to their already scandal-ridden families. Eileen, like all the girls, was a sinner, a daughter of Beelzebub - unless, of course, she repented.

At the end of three years, Eileen Blake returned home a devoutly religious woman. Gone were the rounded freshness of her face and the innocent gaze, replaced by a sharpness of body and eye that made her look twice her age. Now she knew herself to be the sinner they had said she was.

When she saw her son, now aged three, she vowed that she would never be separated from him again.

From the darkness of the room in which Conran Blake had started life, he was taken to live upstairs in the nursery, an arrangement that continued until his mother's death when he was only fifteen. Since he now had no other living relatives, he had attended a succession of boarding schools and summer camps until he was of college age. But strong memories of his good mother had stayed with him. Despite the strict upbringing she had enforced on him, he had loved her. She had been the only real person in his life, the only person he could truly call his own. At least until now.

Conran opened the door, to be met by a welcoming log fire. A food hamper squatted cosily on the floor, and presents he had sent on ahead littered the rug in front of the open fire.

'It's just wonderful, wonderful!' Morgan was saying. 'Oh, Conran, all this for us to share together alone, just you and me! It's unbelievable!'

She ran into his arms. And then, finally, in front of a blazing fire, lying on the sheepskin rug, Morgan Lahiff gave herself to the only man she had ever wanted. The fire created flickering shadows in the dark. Conran ran his hands down her spine. The sensation made her tingle and her hair stand on end. She was delightfully nervous.

How smooth felt the fine contours of her skin, how soft and tender yet firm, how beautifully pale! Her lips met his, softly at first, delicately, just touching. He felt their soft wetness. The warmth from the fire eased her body, so unaccustomed to discovery, yet wanting to be discovered, to be loved for the first time in her life. Now there was no tension, just the faith and security lovers often feel when at one with each other. They were lovers in the garden of Eden. Conran was ecstatic: Cupid himself would have longed to experience the joy that was his. Lying before him was his Aphrodite, his and his alone, to own and to love.

He touched the soft inside of her thigh, drawing his way up to the bridge at the top of her legs. Gently, he introduced his fingers inside her body, to be greeted by the flowing of her secret elixir. Looking into her face, he saw desire alive within the deep green pools that were her eyes. Now, raising his hand, he shared with her the taste of her own arousal. Again his fingers voyaged inside her, deeper, pressing the strength of his love with every touch. His own body had never felt a moment like this, had never been given a moment like this. The perfume of love enhanced their pleasure, igniting a fire deep within each.

Now he supported the small of her back, for, weakened by pleasure, she was almost swooning. Her dazed thoughts sought sanctuary in the warmth of his control. Touching oh so gently, stroking oh so gently, he kissed the swan-like creature beneath him, nuzzling her neck, her stomach, her hips, her thighs. With his tongue, he probed the blonde pubic down, fondled the opening of her womanhood. Her gasp betrayed the delight and pleasure her body felt. In a moment he would enter her and the throb of his penis would be assuaged by blissful release. The sweetness of her drove him faster, while his awareness of her virgin pleasure held his passion back. In this love-making there was no anger and no fear for the future. All was as it should it be.

Twelve gloriously white huskies barked their eagerness to be up and running, pulling behind them the sleigh carrying the two lovers. It was during this ride that Conran Blake and Morgan Lahiff pledged their troth to each other for the rest of their lives.

They spent the rest of the holiday like carefree children, invading the mountains they sledged their way round, building snowmen, hurling snowballs, shrieking with helpless laughter. On Christmas day, Morgan insisted that they attend some sort of religious service, so they found a small church and went to midnight prayers. They dined at home alone, wanting no other company but each other's. Day and night they would make love with a passion that astonished them both. Morgan thought herself the luckiest woman on God's earth. One day she would be the mother of Conran's child. The thought sent her into sheer, delirious delight.

The wedding was planned for July 1st. Conran wanted a large wedding, which conflicted with Morgan's ideas. She wanted a quiet affair, as neither had any family to invite. The few relatives she had in Ireland were too old to make the journey, and the rest had businesses they wouldn't be able to leave in peak season.

They arrived in Manchester slightly subdued at having to leave their little Scottish love nest. Morgan pushed open her flat door, and the cold air rushed the very breath from her. Oh well, back to reality, she thought. Only things would be different from now on, for she was a complete woman in every sense of the word. She had died and been reborn on their trip to Scotland. Mrs Morgan Blake! She said the words out loud, music to the ears.

On New Year's Eve, Morgan and Conran announced their engagement to everyone at the casino. The party was a hot, lavish affair, patronised by all the local dignitaries. Conran introduced each one to Morgan as a business associate. The happy couple's joy flowed as freely as the champagne. But consuming too much champagne always has to be paid for afterwards...

Hilary showed delight at the news, and her pleasure seemed genuine. This puzzled Morgan, for Hilary, who was her supervisor, had always been quite aloof, not showing much interest in her young charge. Yet, as far as Morgan knew, Hilary and Conran had a good business relationship; they worked well together, and Hilary was loyal and dependable. Perhaps she was simply the quiet motherly type, who was overcome by such occasions.

'Morgan, I'm so pleased for you both,' Hilary was saying now. 'You must let me have the wedding list.'

'Thanks, Hilary, it's nice of you to share our happiness.'

'Conran, what can I say? Your future wife is very beautiful.'

But Hilary was far from happy. In fact, anger was welling up inside her like a pressure cooker ready to blow. An Irish bitch! Of all the girls in the casino, he'd chosen that Irish gold-digger. Well, she wouldn't have it, she certainly would not! Finding an excuse to leave the party early (something about problems with the baby-sitter), she drove home, tears of loathing rolling down her pinched face.

When she reached home, she went through the front door of her council house and found the baby-sitter in the living room.

'Matty, you can go now. Is she asleep?'

'Yes, Miss.'

'Here, take this - and there's a bit extra for a cab. I don't need you to stay over tonight. Thanks, Matty.'

Matty, a local girl, had never seen Hilary in quite such a sombre mood as this. Somehow she didn't like to leave her.

'Are you okay, Miss? You look a bit pale. Is there something I can get you?'

'No, I'm fine, just tired. Tell your mum I'll call round tomorrow.'

The door slammed and Hilary was alone. Pouring herself a scotch, she ran her fingers along the gilt-edged photo frame that stood proudly on the drinks cabinet.

'Peter. Oh Peter, I miss you so much!' she sobbed quietly. 'Things would have been so different if you'd lived. I would never have got involved in… everything. My life would have been spent taking care of you, providing a home for you and me. We had such a short time together. If they'd left us alone, we would have been okay. For sure we would.'

CHAPTER SIX

From infancy to early adolescence, Hilary Nugent's family life had been productive and stable. In those days her father had been as every father should be. Fred Nugent was very much in love with his wife Anna, and she with him, and they both doted on their family. When Anna discovered a small lump in her breast, she thought nothing of it and did not seek the advice of her doctor.

Anna Nugent's death was all the more tragic because it could have been prevented. Fred bore his loss badly. He was a broken man. At the tender age of thirteen, Hilary swore to keep the family together and take up the role her mother had left. Peter, her six-year-old brother, could not understand why his mother was not around any more.

The headstrong Hilary did indeed become the mother Peter so badly needed, providing all the care and attention Anna would have lavished on them both. As womanhood wrought its hormonal changes, Hilary, her hands full, did not stop to think of herself or her future. Keeping the family together remained her only concern.

Fred Nugent, meanwhile, had started to drink. He began to spend less time with his children. The numbing effects of the whisky on his memory enticed him to drink more and more. He would stagger through the front door around eleven-thirty every night, reeking of alcohol.

On this particular night Hilary had stayed up late to finish some mending. She had not heard her father come in, so she was not aware of him standing in the living room doorway, his eyes trying to focus on her. Sitting there in front of the hearth, she could almost have been his Anna. How like her mother his daughter looked in every way: dark features, black eyes, oh, and her body, now becoming so womanly, so much like the woman Anna had been. Fred wondered if he touched her, would she feel like his wife, would it feel the same?

Hilary gasped as she felt a hand stroke the back of her neck. 'I didn't hear you come in, Dad!'

He did not answer. Hilary felt faintly uneasy. Perhaps it was the strange look in his eyes as he peered down at her. Ready for bed after her long day, Hilary said goodnight to her father, but still he did not respond. He simply continued to stare at her.

Up in her room, Hilary hitched up her long cotton nightdress and climbed into bed. Turning out the light, she pondered on the strangeness of her dad's behaviour. She really wished he would give up the drink, even though she knew it temporarily blotted out his suffering. How many nights had she heard his muffled cries as he cursed the Lord for taking his beautiful wife?

On this night she could hear no crying. The house was still. Hilary was on the verge of sleep when she heard the turn of the door handle. It was dark that first night Fred Nugent climbed into his daughter's bed. She had not been sure what her daddy wanted, but it felt unreal as he massaged the small bumps that were her breasts, then took hold of her nightdress and pulled it up to her waist, murmuring promises not to hurt her.

For all her youth, Hilary knew that this was not normal, that her father should not be doing these things to her, which made her sore in certain places. These were things that only mummies and daddies did together. Still, it would have to be okay, as she was the mother now, wasn't she? And if she did not tell anyone, then the three of them could stay together.

In the safety of the dark, Fred Nugent would play games with his daughter - the kind of games only daddies could play with their daughters. He was losing his mind. Every day, a little more madness took charge of him. Hilary became his wife, his Anna, who had always allowed him any pleasure. Anna, who had known how to please a man in every way. No matter what form his sexual demands took, the girl withstood the nightly intrusion. After all, he was never rough with her, and sometimes he would use soothing ointments, especially when he asked her to turn over on to her stomach.

The internal damage wasn't too serious, but enough to make her collapse during a PE session at school. Waking up surrounded by doctors, her legs wide apart and straddled in stirrups, Hilary felt humiliated and ashamed. What were they doing to her, and why was she here? Staring around at the men and nurses in masks, Hilary was subjected to a medical examination that would have humiliated even the most experienced of mothers. As they pushed and probed inside her young body, she realised it must have something to do with the things her father did to her at night. Hating herself for being so weak, she took the blame for what followed. Social services were on the case before she'd even got out of the hospital. She never returned to the home she'd known, but went straight into her first care hostel. And Peter wasn't there.

She was shown to a room adequately furnished, yet dismal. An array of coloured felt-tip pen marks adorned the walls, the legacy of the previous juvenile tenant. How had her clothes and belongings got there, and why weren't they at home where they should be?

A social worker visited her that same evening. The interview was strained, and Hilary felt aggressive towards this busybody who had torn the life out of her family. Her first question to the stony-faced, prissy woman concerned the whereabouts of her little brother. The answer told Hilary nothing; she was informed simply that Peter was safe. From then on, the interview mainly focused on her father and the goings-on in the family home. Hilary did not want to answer these intrusive questions about her dad. After all, she loved him as the last adult member of her family.

'When can I see my dad?'

'I'm afraid that's not possible.'

'But I want to see him!'

The social worker, a shallow, heartless woman, felt nothing but revulsion for the girl. How could she possibly want to stay in contact with that filthy pervert of a father? The woman had no understanding, no sympathy for the situation. Maybe, she thought maliciously, the kid had even enjoyed the sex. Could she not see that, to Hilary, despite what Fred had done to her, she loved him with the same love any child instinctively feels for its father? After all, he had kept his children safe, fed and clothed. He'd read to them, taken them to the park, done all the things a father does. He was, and always would be, Hilary's dad, no matter what. The ties of blood were so much stronger than this obtuse woman could fathom.

Now she tried a different tack. 'Hilary, why don't you tell me about Peter? Did daddy ever play games with Peter like he did with you?'

Although only fifteen, the girl was bright and knew instantly what this hard-nosed social worker was getting at.

'No, never! Do you think I would allow anyone to touch my brother? Don't you understand that's why I ... Where is he?'

'Calm yourself, you've been through a great deal.'

'I want my family back! I want my family back! I want to go home. What have you done to my dad? Where's Peter? You *bitch*, you fucking stupid *bitch*!'

Hate and hysteria rose like venom in the soul of this wretched child. She tore through the room, knocking down anything that got in her way. Running after her, the social worker called her name. Hilary turned and saw the woman's face awash with fear. *She* was the reason why Hilary was now alone, and why everything she loved had been taken away.

Suddenly, the social worker fell to the floor with the impact of Hilary's sharp left hook. Grabbing her hair, Hilary repeatedly banged the woman's head on the floor until blood flowed. The woman screamed for help, which soon came in the form of two butch women dressed in overalls.

'Right, that's enough, Miss Nugent, that's quite enough of that!'

Holding onto the door jamb, this representative of decent society tried to regain some measure of dignity, before darting from the building as though the devil himself was on her heels. It was said that she resigned soon after the confrontation.

Back in the room, having been severely reprimanded, the misunderstood teenager cried herself to sleep.

The call of the dawn rose with the scent of summer's dew lingering on the flowers, which Hilary could see from her window. All was peace and quiet. The world was still. This would be the perfect time for her to start her search for Peter and her father. The night duty staff were still fast asleep in their beds, and Hilary found it easy to prise open the lock on the office door. In no time she had found her file and was searching quickly for the information that would tell her where she could find her family.

It looked good. Less than two miles away, Peter was being held at a hostel not unlike the one in which she was incarcerated. Right! She would find what was hers and take it back. Then she would find her dad, and they would all go home. Although, deep inside, she knew it wasn't quite that simple, she did not want to believe it, so she soldered on in her quest.

Then, at the bottom of the first page she read: '*Fred Nugent held in custody until trial, on suspicion of child abuse. Nature of abuse: sexual. Conviction expected.*' The word *conviction, conviction* kept going round in her head till she could no longer bear to think of what might happen to her father.

Thank God it was summer. With a little luck the weather would stay warm. That would make running away easier, especially for little Peter. After all, she intended to care for Peter in the same protective manner she always had since losing her mother.

A petty cash box was tucked inside the filing cabinet. It really was very easy.

The building was still, almost deathlike. Its white, forbidding walls suggested a sanatorium or prison rather than a home for kids. How was she to get in? Maybe she wouldn't need to. Perhaps if she waited, she could grab Peter when he came out. Well, they would have to let him out some time.

Marched out like toy soldiers, each dressed in identical hats, coats and scarves, the boys set off for school. Peter was the fourth to emerge, looking pale and lost. A bus was waiting at the end of the drive, and it was here that Hilary beckoned to Peter, miming to him to keep quiet. She was overwhelmed with joy that she had found her little brother, and wept silently as she hugged him to her chest. Peter's reaction was that of a child on Christmas morning: all wide-eyed amazement.

'Are we going to get daddy and go home now?' he whispered.

She nodded. Then, oblivious to the shouts of the care workers, who had suddenly realised what was going on, they ran and ran till they reached the station.

Hilary had no idea where they could go, but they would have to get away fast, as the authorities would already be alerted. They boarded a train to Liverpool and, once there, gorged themselves on a breakfast of crisps and fizzy drinks. Until darkness fell, they wandered around the shops and parks. Peter played on the swings, giggling and unaware that anything was really wrong. But eventually he grew restless.

'Can we go home now?' he insisted.

'No, we're on an adventure,' Hilary said conspiratorially. 'You can't just leave in the middle of an adventure. I know, let's stay out all night. Dad won't mind. He knows you're with me. What do you say?'

'Yes, we can pretend we're soldiers in the army!'

'That's right.'

They bedded down for the night by Liverpool docks. The air still held the warmth of the day, so they weren't cold. Half-hidden beneath a pile of boxes, Peter slept soundly while Hilary planned their next move.

But daylight brought the unwelcome attention of a security guard, who had just woken up in time not to be caught dozing on the job by his superior. The sight of the two huddled, sleeping youngsters was so pitiful, he felt a lump in his throat. Not wanting to wake them, the well-meaning guard simply called the police, who came and took them away.

Hilary was sent to a secure home - not exactly a borstal, but not exactly a care hostel. They said she was violent. Peter was fostered to a nice, middle-class childless couple in Standish, a town way outside Manchester, in the country. Their father was given a long prison sentence.

At sixteen Hilary was given back her liberty. By this time, she could swear with the best of them, fight with the best of them , and fuck with the best of them. Yet her main ambition was to be reunited with her beloved brother, who was now nine. For this she would need her own home. She needed money, yet what little the dole paid wouldn't even pay for the train fare to Standish.

She was allowed a half-hour visit every week. The Wards, Peter's foster parents, made her very welcome and offered her tea. That was nice. At least they were looking after him well. In fact, Peter was doing more than well; he had a stable, loving home. The Wards gave him everything a young boy could wish for, including affection.. Here Peter would grow up to be a well-adjusted young man, complete with a sense of morality. And he brought his foster parents great joy. Hilary's meeting with him was emotional. Peter hadn't forgotten his sister by any means; here, in front of him, stood a part of his very recent yet very different past.

Soon Hilary found a job - of sorts. Being on the game wasn't so bad. She liked the money, if not the customers. She saved and saved, hoping to get a nice flat with a room for Peter when he was old enough to leave the Wards' care and move in with her. It would be just like old times; knowing she had someone to love injected fuel into her life.

Time passed quickly for Peter, and he grew into a nice, decent young lad. He was ambitious, and had chosen the army as his future career. Hilary took the news badly, knowing it would mean long periods of separation.

'Look, Hill,' Peter assured her as they sat in the lovely flat she had managed to find. 'I'll still be coming home, you know. It's the army, not a prison sentence! So keep my room for me - this is my home now. When I think of all the hours you've put in at that supermarket to provide me with all this - well!'

'What about the Wards? Will you go home to them?'

'Of course I'll go and see them. I love them, they've done so much for me. But you're my sister and always will be, and my home's with you. You'll see.'

So Peter became a fine, upstanding and much-travelled member of the British Army. Hilary cherished his visits home. At these times, she would stop her street work and tell her brother she had holidays due from the supermarket, which she had saved for his visits. They went on days out together, laughed and had fun, making up for a childhood that they rarely spoke about now. The subject of their father was never mentioned. It was as if both refused to invite the past in to wreak havoc on any chance they might have of a normal future. Yet in theirs minds, he was not forgotten - just put in a box with the lid securely locked.

Even so, Hilary bore many scars from the past. Time could not erase the deep-rooted pain and humiliation of her experiences. She carried the truth of her life around with her. But to the outside world, she appeared strong, resilient. She needed no one except Peter. Should he fall in love with someone, what then? Well, she'd think about that when the time came. For now, it was okay. All Peter talked about was his career. The boy was bright, it was obvious, and he was already on his way to an exciting career. Hilary was so proud of him, it made everything worthwhile. Yet haunting her happiness was the prospect of Peter finding out about her involvement with prostitution and, more recently, drug trafficking.

When Peter announced that he was going to Northern Ireland, Hilary felt cold and numb. That day someone walked over her grave.

'Don't be silly, Hill. I'll be okay. God, it's not half as bad as the media makes out, honest. I'll be doing no more than helping old ladies across the road.'

Had he deliberately made light of it? Well, how could he tell her the truth? For the truth was that plans had been made to infiltrate an IRA active service unit, and he had been specially chosen for the mission. It was his chance for promotion, a step up the ladder. At such a prospect, danger was something an ambitious young soldier would take in his stride.

What was left of Peter came home in a box. Hilary threw the bearer of the terrible news out of the house, refusing the offer of company to help to ease the blow. At about twelve o'clock that night, Hilary released a heart-rending, wretched cry, a cry that could be heard at the end of the street. It was a cry of utter despair.

The funeral was beyond mournful - just a few people, including the Wards, at a low-key service. Hilary had become furious at the suggestion of an army funeral. Peter hadn't died a hero in her eyes. He had been murdered by the Irish, and duped by his own kind, the army, into thinking he was something special, when all the time they had used him.

The Wards, who had wanted Peter buried with military honours, knew not to argue with Hilary, and decided that she had the right to make the decision. She would not let them pay for the funeral either. No, he was hers, or had been, hadn't he? They had merely been his guardians for a few years. Peter was her business.

Standing by the graveside, her thoughts were lost in death. From every angle, spasms of anguish ravaged both her body and her mind. Grey with grief, she looked far older than her years but she didn't care.

She waited till everyone had gone. It was cold and getting dark, but at least she was alone. Throwing herself down on Peter's grave, she began to dig and dig and dig with her bare hands.

'No, Peter. No, please don't …don't… leave me… for God's sake, not you. I need you…'

Stopping in a moment of lucid realisation, she looked up at the stars, her finger stained with dirt. Reaching out to nobody, Hilary in many ways died that night.

Nothing was left for her now but to make money. She was going big time. First, she'd get her priorities right. Give up the street game, go into dealing more. There were whores who would pay her to protect them, show them the way. It would be worth their while.

Did they think that she would allow Peter... no, she meant Conran... to marry that murdering Irish bitch and live happily ever after? It would be a cold day in hell before that happened, and that was exactly where she intended to send sweet Miss Innocent.

Conran had great aspirations for the children Morgan would bear him. He had planned many sons. Morgan wanted the same, but added a daughter to the list. Each child would be perfection itself. Perhaps they should reserve a place now at the best schools? After all, such things were important.

So, the wedding was set, everything was going according to plan. True, there had been some friction when Conran finally came clean about owning the casino. In fact, Morgan was livid at first. Yet, as her now good friend Hilary said, it had all been done for the finest of reasons.

'Come on, Morgan, don't take it to heart,' Hilary had urged. 'When he met you he saw you were in a spot and he knew that he could help. It's obvious why he didn't want to tell you. He knew you would never have taken the job.'

'I don't like deceit, Hilary. In any form.'

'Does it matter now? He loves you.'

And so Morgan was placated. In Hilary she had found someone wise, even maternal, whom she could trust; someone who knew Conran nearly as well as she did herself. Yes, Hilary was a Godsend.

As the wedding approached, there was yet another fitting for the wedding dress, a plain, medieval peasant-style gown, that clung tightly to the body. A headdress made from real bark entwined with white heather completed the enchanting look.

'Have you put on weight?' scolded Mrs Jarvis, the dressmaker. 'I think I'm going to have to let it out a bit. Any more weight, my girl, and you'll be on a strict diet.'

Suddenly, a realisation flooded Morgan's thoughts. No! Add two and two together - no period this month and last. Oh, bloody hell!

Again, Hilary came to the rescue. 'Look, just go and take the test. It's not such a catastrophe, you'll be married soon.'

'Sodding hell, Hilary, I'll look like an elephant walking down the aisle!'

The test confirmed her fears.

But Conran was over the moon. It was decided that Morgan would move into the house straight away, instead of waiting for the wedding, which is what she had actually wanted. Yet she was rather glad. The bedsit had begun to get on her nerves after spending so much time with Conran in the big house at Orrell. En-suite bathrooms and constant hot water, initially a luxury, were now becoming almost a necessity.

Everything went well for the first few weeks. It was almost as good as Scotland.

Then, one day, Morgan had been shopping in town and lost all track of time. On the way home, the traffic was horrendous, and it was six-thirty before she arrived back at the house. Conran was already home. Parking the white BMW, which he had bought her as an early wedding present, in the large drive, she rushed out of the car, almost dropping her shopping. He liked her to be home when he got in from work, and today he was very disappointed to find the house empty.

He'd had a shit day. The new consignment of amphetamines was cut to fuck with glucose - so much for the dealer he'd started. His contact at the dockside had been busted and over twenty grand of coke lost. Fuck, did he have to baby-sit these people? Why couldn't anybody do their job right? He paid them enough. The thought of going home to his woman had kept him going.

Morgan dived through the front door, dropping her bags in the spacious Victorian hall. Conran was waiting at the bottom of the staircase. He had just polished off his fourth scotch.

'Where the fuck have you been?'

Morgan was about to apologise until she heard the tone of his voice.

'Sorry, are you talking to me?'

'I said where the fuck have you been?'

'Well, Conran, I would have thought it was obvious, but if it's too complicated for you to work out, then I'll explain.'

Things started to grow dark. The familiar tension threatened to explode inside his head. Placing his glass on the floor and dropping the butt of his cigarette into it, he walked towards her. Morgan headed for the kitchen, almost reaching the large brass handle, until the feel of his hand on her throat pulled her back. He slammed her against the wall and held his face close to hers.

'Don't. Just don't ever talk down to me, do you understand?'

For the first time, Morgan was afraid of her future husband, but she was damned if she was going to show it. After all, she was Irish.

'Take your hands off me now,'

The slap hurt and made her dizzy. For a moment or two she held her own. Then, all at once, Conran backed off, the reality of what he was doing suddenly gripping him. This wasn't one of his tarts; this was his woman, the woman he was going to marry...

Morgan had made it to the top of the stairs, feeling the need to lie down before she could put his actions into perspective.

CHAPTER SEVEN

The next day, Morgan was still in turmoil. She had heard stories about wife battering, but she found she couldn't dwell on them now. What do you do when you love someone so much, you can't just pack a bag and leave? When you love someone so much they are your life, your thoughts, your breath? God, how could you just leave like that? Then again, how many blows did you put up with? Was there a specific limit? Her heart told her that this was a one-off. To leave would be ridiculous.

Or was she making excuses for him? No, she thought: to hell with leaving the man she loved. She unpacked the small hand luggage she had prepared in the first flush of anger. Could the baby be hurt? No, that was a horrible thought, it wasn't as though he'd punched her or anything. It had just been a slap. Conran would never hurt her baby.

Around two o'clock, a bang on the front door made her stomach turn over. It was Hilary.

'Conran sent you, didn't he, Hilary?'

'Does it matter? It got me off work anyway,' she said with a smile.

'Look, Hill, I'm not in the mood for company.'

'Sorry, I must have been mistaken when I thought we were friends. Oh well, you can never tell a person, eh?'

With that Hilary turned to walk away. So the Irish bitch didn't want to talk! Oh, poor little girlie! Did she get a nasty smack off daddy? Oh dear, dear! Well, Hilary hadn't volunteered to go round. He'd sent her, straight after she'd given him one hell of a blow job. Ah, if the bitch only knew!

Morgan was repentant. 'Hill, I'm sorry. Come on I'll put the kettle on.'

'Sod the kettle, let's have a real drink.'

'You know I can't, but there's nothing stopping you.'

Hilary produced a bottle of Bourbon from her handbag, a little thank you gift from the boss. Once again, she eased Morgan's mind, talked her out of making a big deal of things. By the time Conran returned early that evening, Hilary was just preparing to leave.

His apology was genuine and humble. Morgan had to put it all behind her, they must start afresh, maybe both try a little harder. Promise to talk more, explain what they expected of each other. Then they would be as happy as before.

The wedding reception was lavish, the catering excellent, the stately home a wonderful venue. The bride and groom looked like they belonged on the front cover of Vogue, and the guests were suitably glamorous, including Hilary, who looked chic in a grey-blue two-piece suit. Morgan's uncle had not been able to make the occasion, but he sent his best regards.

Morgan gave birth on November 11th to a baby boy weighing six pounds and seven ounces. They called him Stewart. The birth was difficult, leaving her weak and fragile. Still, with a good rest and the right medication, all would be well.

After two weeks in hospital, Morgan couldn't wait for Conran to take them home - the proud father carrying his wife and new-born son into his own private kingdom. Since Morgan was still weak, Conran had decided that Hilary should move into the house for a while, until his wife felt stronger. This did not please Morgan. What was he saying? That she wasn't capable of looking after her own child? She didn't want Hilary, despite all her kindness, moving in with them. And anyway, what about her own daughter, Tanya?

The problem was soon resolved. Tanya was to have a child-minder. Morgan tried to tell Conran that she wanted them to be alone as a family, but then she thought herself selfish. After all, he was only taking care of her and Stewart.

The child became Conran's very existence. He cooed over

him and pulled funny faces at him in his cot. Hilary watched the scene with distaste. The baby was, after all, the spawn of an Irish whore, worth nothing.

Morgan was soon back to health, eager to perform her role as the perfect mother. Despite her gratitude for Hilary's help, she longed to be rid of her house guest. But how could she now ask Hilary to leave? She simply couldn't.

Each day Hilary observed the Blake family, resenting their happiness. If Peter had lived, then maybe she too could have known the feeling of true happiness. No, anything she had ever loved had been taken from her. Yet still others rammed their sickly contentment in your face. Isn't that what they were doing? Why hadn't Conran told her to leave, now she was no longer needed? It must be that he was teasing her, showing off. Was she losing her position and was he losing respect for her?

The thought of losing the man made her stomach turn somersaults and her head go dizzy. To be rejected again! No, no, it would not happen. That bastard child was not going to steal Conran like the Celtic whore had. The schemer had stolen her place, taken something she loved and made her no better than a hired hand, when it should have been her as mistress of the house. She saw to Conran's real needs, needs which came late at night and were fulfilled in the safety of the room at the bottom of the house where no one ever went. There, little Miss could not hear them. There they could be alone.

Yet once their intimate encounter was over and she no longer played the mother role, Hilary knew she was nothing more than a servant to him, a useful presence to take care of his delicate wife. Resentment grew and she tried to control it with her will, but it was almost impossible. The sight of Morgan, the sound of Morgan and Conran sharing what should have been hers to share with him. The bitch was coming between her and Conran and any future happiness she could hope for. Now the fucking kid was just something else to ease her out of her rightful place. Well, this time she meant to do something about it. It was time to deal her own hand and play a little god.

CHAPTER EIGHT

Stewart was now three months old and showed all the signs of a contented baby: he was growing fast, feeding well, and developing his own charm. His eyes were alert, his hair abundant, his fingers deliciously plump. He was forever emitting soft whispering gurgles, which delighted Morgan. Conran was convinced that the child had uttered 'Da-da'; Morgan laughed at such a thought, but was touched by her husband's wishful thinking.

Only one person failed to be charmed by the new arrival...

Sleeping pills were easily obtained. In fact, the whole thing had been easy. With mummy and daddy fast asleep, Hilary crept from her room and into the old nursery where the creature lay. Staring into the cot at the happy infant, she had hatred in her eyes and a burning evil in her veins. The breathing of the infant echoed in her head, its smiling face seeming to laugh at her. The poignant smell of baby reviled her nostrils. Even this thing, so small, so helpless, mocked her. It had to die.

Reaching into the crib and taking hold of the fluffy pillow, Hilary stretched her arms into the air. The child's eyes opened just as the pillow put him back to sleep - a sleep he would not wake from.

It was Morgan who found the dead baby. Conran, distraught, screamed and blamed his wife for neglecting the child; in her grief, she accused him. Nobody thought to blame good old Hilary, especially after the inquest, at which the verdict was cot death.

Their grief was devastating for everyone to see - except Hilary, who considered she had done no more than mete out justice. Yet she still craved more.

Conran threw himself into his work. He became a monster to anyone who crossed his path. He took on more men, doubled the size of his empire, setting up a bigger kingdom in which to hide. And just that little bit of coke saw him through the day.

Morgan was pitiful. Soon even Mrs Atkinson, the housekeeper, expressed concern, hinting that the young wife was in need of help of the psychiatric kind. Since the death of baby Stewart, Morgan had taken to wandering around the house in a helpless daze, clutching the shawl she used to wrap the child in. She could smell him, he was still with her. Now painfully thin and wan, her hair lank and unwashed, eyes dull and listless, Morgan was no longer the beauty she had once been.

As time passed, things did not improve. Sitting around the house all day doing nothing was not helping the situation any, and Conran was losing patience with his wife.

Today saw him home early for a change. He found Morgan still in her nightgown sitting in front of the TV, watching nothing in particular, still clutching the little shawl. It was a familiar sight.

'You look a fucking mess!' he said brutally.

She paid no attention to him. What did she care how she looked? She had failed as a mother and a wife. What was there left?

'Did you hear me? Get dressed.' He could take no more. How long was this going to go on for? 'Put that bloody shawl down. Do you think you are the only one that's grieving, the only one that hurts? I've suffered for the both of us.'

'He was my child, *my child*!' screamed Morgan. 'How can I go on now?'

'What about me?' Conran yelled back. 'Don't I count? I'm still here, not that you'd notice. When was the last time we went out? The last time we made love?'

'What did I do wrong? Was it something I did? Could I have been a better mother? How? Why? I need to know. *Why*?'

'Shut up! *Shut the fuck up*! Get dressed.'

'Please don't shout at me, Conran,' Morgan whimpered. Still she clutched the shawl tightly.

'We're going out this evening.'

'No.'

'Yes, like any other normal couple. Go and get dressed. Do something with yourself, for God's sake!'

'You go, I'm staying home.'

Conran couldn't take any more. His head was about to explode with the old pains again.

It happened so quickly. The blow sent her sprawling on the floor and the shawl that had belonged to his dead son sent thick black smoke up the chimney as it burnt. Morgan's outrage was animalistic. It startled him. She tore at his face, ripping her nails into his flesh, pulling and digging deep into his skin with all the strength of a wild beast.

'I hate you, I *hate* you!' she screamed. 'I'll kill you for this, I'll kill you! That was all I had left of my son.'

She kicked and fought in a pure frenzy. Conran was shocked at her strength. I must calm her, he kept saying to himself. This he did by a blow that put her out for the rest of the evening.

The next morning, when she came round, Morgan realised how bad she has become, how her grief and guilt had consumed her totally. It was hard to admit that she needed help but, for the sake of her marriage, she decided to seek medical advice.

Hilary revelled in the marks of war left on Conran's face. So the cat had claws, eh? But to Conran she showed understanding and the comfort he craved. Surely this would be the bitch's final downfall. Hilary smiled to herself. How she looked forward to the day she and Peter would be alone together once again. She checked herself. Conran... She meant, Conran. It was a slip of the tongue.

The psychiatrist was good. After many consultations, he finally got Morgan to realise that cot death was not the fault of the parents. It was something that just happened. He also made her realise that locking herself away in grief would change nothing. She had a life to live, a husband to love. It was time to leave the past and work for the future, for her marriage.

Slowly she improved. She and Conran started to make love again, at first more for his sake, but gradually she came back to life, a phoenix rising from the ashes. Of course she never forgot her first-born, but all was well again - or as well as it could be.

Justin Edwards had come into the employment of Conran Blake via Carol, one of his female conquests who had remained a good friend. Carol had worked alongside Justin when they were both croupiers on a cruise ship, before staying in England to get married and taking at job at the casino. She was not one of Conran's special employees, knowing nothing of his alternative business.

Justin was young, handsome and intelligent, with all the charm and vitality of youth. It would be true to say he had a touch of the rogue in him, though it was the loveable kind. Nothing was ever serious to Justin - he simply lived and loved. Many a female had fallen for his boyish charm; yet, to be fair to him, he had never misled any of his lovers, always taking pains to make it clear that he was in it just for the fun and friendship - strictly short-term. It was impossible to dislike Justin.

His last semi-serious love affair had been on board the Canberra, entertaining a rich, attractive middle-aged colonel's wife called Margery, who was bored waiting for the return of her husband. She had taken a cruise to alleviate her boredom, and Justin had certainly done that. He'd made her happy and, if he was honest, he'd grown fond of her too. But when she offered him residence at her stately home, he had decided it was time to leave. Being the puppy of a rich older woman was not his style. They parted on good terms, both equally satisfied with the fun they'd had.

Finally, when jumping from ship to ship got tiring, Justin decided that it was time to stay in good old Blighty - for a while at least.

The casino had undergone huge renovations, and a new room had been added. The grand re-opening night approached. Conran and Morgan were now settled back down together and trying desperately to have another baby. They both looked forward to the opening. All staff had been supplied with suitable evening attire. Morgan, who had regained some weight, wore a lavish off-the-shoulder gown, royal blue trimmed with gold edging, which hugged her tightly, enhancing her figure. The dress had a long slash at the hip, allowing her elegant legs to be tastefully shown. She wore her hair up for the occasion, sprinkled here and there with blue diamonds to set off her mass of blonde hair, which was swept around her head, Audrey Hepburn-style. Her slender neck and white skin perfectly set off the blue diamond-studded choker Conran had bought her specially for the occasion. Conran himself wore a loose-fitting cream evening suit made of pure silk, and his eyes glittered with the shot of cocaine he had taken earlier.

They made their entrance, greeted by loud applause. People could not help but stare at the gorgeous couple as they drifted by on a cloud of sophistication. And the guests were equally glamorous: TV and film stars lit up the room, giving a Hollywood feel to the occasion, and VIPs sipped champagne in clusters. Business was going well, as people were playing the tables with flair, careless of the huge losses they made. Morgan thought it vulgar how they threw their money around so conspicuously. Was it really necessary, she murmured to Conran, to be so obvious with one's wealth? He just kissed her and laughed.

'Darling, they're having fun, can't you see that? They're just making the most of this economic boom Manchester's enjoying. Why don't you go and find Hilary? You haven't seen her all evening. Run along, darling, while I talk business.'

Hilary had her hands full overseeing the female staff, checking internal security systems and keeping an eye on things in general. She looked regal in a long black evening gown, the diamante earrings and necklace that Conran had bought for her sparkling at her ears and throat.

'Got time for a drink, H?' Morgan asked her.

'You've got to be kidding, with all the new staff to look after. Why, are you bored? Go have a dance with Conran.'

'He's busy talking finance, as always. Maybe I'll go on my own. See you later.'

Morgan loved music and the sound of the Drifters made her feet itch to dance. It had been a long time since she'd danced the night away, and the prospect was delicious.

Justin Edwards had missed the grand entrance of the Blake's. His attention had been focused upon the sassy little blond who had been attending the bar opposite his table. Now it was time for his break and perhaps time to do a little girlie watching.

'Here, let me get this for you,' he offered.

Morgan turned and smiled at the handsome young man behind her. 'No, really, that's okay.'

'The music's great isn't it?'

'Yes it is. You obviously work here.'

'Well, the uniform's a bit of a giveaway. I'm new. So far I'm enjoying it. What do you do?'

Morgan's long absence from the casino after Stewart's death, and the fact that he had just started, meant Justin was not aware of who she was. She realised she liked the anonymity. He was so easy to talk to, and for the next half hour they chatted and danced, until Hilary had to find him and tell him in no uncertain terms to get back to the tables.

Hilary, whose duties now extended to the hiring and firing of all the Croupiers, had been annoyed at the unprofessional behaviour of this new member of staff. But then, catching sight of Morgan's embarrassed expression, she thought again.

'Hilary, it was my fault really. I just kept on dancing. I'm sure he thought it would be rude to leave a lady alone on the dance floor.'

'Oh, no harm done. Come on, Conran's looking for you.'

Conran was slightly impatient but not really annoyed at her absence. Greeting her, he introduced her to the Mayor and Mayoress, and escorted them all to the crap tables, where Morgan smiled in recognition at the handsome croupier.

Justin, meanwhile, had almost died when he saw Conran approach, his arm round Morgan, and realised that he'd been dancing with the boss's wife. Yet, despite his sense of impending danger, he couldn't help trying to get close to her at the table.

Conran was nobody's fool. He saw the young pup flirting with his wife, but didn't really blame him: Morgan was, after all, a beautiful woman. What he didn't like was the way his wife was flirting back and coming on twice as strong.

The evening came to an end. All goodbyes were said and then Gregory Scott drove them home. The fight started in the car.

'You made a complete idiot of yourself tonight!' Conran barked.

'Oh darling, you'd know of course, being an authority on idiots,' Morgan retorted. 'Anyway, why is that? Do tell me.'

'You think I didn't notice you fooling around with the new croupier? It would have been hard not to. Do you want to fuck him?'

Morgan was shocked and hurt by the statement, yet she refused to pacify him.

'No, do you?'

The punch caught her off guard as her head banged against the door.

'You bastard!'

'Fucking dirty bitch, you're all the same. Well, say goodbye to lover boy because tomorrow he's fired.'

Oh God, what had she done? She'd been a fool to play around in that way: she should have known that it would be Justin who suffered. How thoughtless she had been in a moment of folly; now she'd put the innocent guy on the dole.

Although it grieved her, she had to crawl to Conran just to get Justin off the hook. She was woman enough and soon had him eating out of her hand. Yet for every blow he struck, every empty promise that it would never happen again, she found it that little bit harder to love him as she once had.

Back home, the coffee was ready and Morgan poured herself a much needed cup before heading for the stairs to bed.

Conran appeared behind her, his face thunderous. 'Isn't there one for me?'

'Please, Conran, no more tonight. I'm tired. You've made your point, okay? I've said I'm sorry. What more can I do? What's wrong? Didn't you hit me hard enough? Do you want to hit me again?'

'Deny you deserve it!'

'For God's sake!'

Hoping he wouldn't follow too soon, at least till she'd had time to fall asleep, Morgan sat in front of the dressing table, dabbing at the cut on her lip.

Meanwhile, Conran was in the living room, nursing a whisky and silently fuming. Why did he always feel like he was in the wrong? As though she was superior to him in all things. Why did he feel small when she spoke to him in that way? She was his wife and it was her job to make him feel good, to feel like a man, not a naughty child. Fucking bitch thought she was better than him. Well, he'd sort her out once and for all, get this marriage on the right track, make her understand who wore the trousers. And tonight would be the night.

He entered the bedroom and watched as she pampered her face.

'Come away from the mirror. I didn't harm that pretty face, not like I could have done.'

'Don't Conran, just don't carry this on.'

She was scared. Her immediate thought was not to antagonise him, knowing that he was not in the mood to be pushed. Conran could see the fear in her eyes. Was he finally getting through to her?

'Look, Conran, it's been a long night for all of us. Let's get some sleep, we can talk in the morning.'

'Are you sure you want *me* here, not lover boy? I can arrange it for you.'

Her stomach lurched. He was really on a mission, and not going to let go easily. His eyes glittered with a strangely controlled expression: not anger, but something more contrived - more dangerous.

'I don't want him. I want *you*. I've only ever wanted you,' she said, gazing at him through the reflection in the mirror.

'Do you, my darling wife? Do you really want me? Really *want* me?'

'Of course I do.'

'Then come to me.'

There was no choice now. To refuse would have meant disaster. She would have to go to him and play the worshipping wife.

He reached into the folds of her blonde hair and released it from the hair grips. It tumbled softly down her back. How like a treasure it felt - *she* felt! His beautiful wife: could he ever lose this, that he held in his arms, that was so dear to him?

Pulling away, he instructed her to remove her clothes. 'Take your dress off.'

She did so, weeping inwardly. This was so unlike the loving that had begun their relationship. His desire was so cold, so empty now.

'Lie on the bed and beg me to love you.'

'Conran, I can't.'

'You don't love me. You lied.'

'No.'

So, helpless, she followed his instructions, suffering the mental humiliation. Her hatred for him was almost tangible now.

Holding her, he pressed his hardness against her, rubbing up and down, touching her breast, diving into her soft opening. He entered her, but she was dry land and not at all welcoming. For though she could pretend with words, her body could not lie.

From the drawer he took a length of rope and proceeded

to tie her to the bedpost, face down. The impression he gave at first was that it was a game, yet as he tied the ropes tighter, panic rushed through her thoughts. He had her spread-eagled now, all her limbs bound.

'No, Conran, not like this! I can't love you like this.'

'This has nothing to do with loving, my dearest wife. This is your punishment and my right, as I now own you. You belong to me. It is for me to punish you, because you have sinned. Have you not?'

He ran his fingers down her spine, then covered her with all his weight and strength. He kissed her neck and felt the fear in her body, relishing it. Who was high and mighty now? Who controlled whom? Who was the man now? He entered her, moving slowly, then more vigorously. She made no moan of response or encouragement. She was silent. Damn her, he thought. He would make her scream. Now was the time to introduce his wife to some real sins of the flesh.

Now, half-crazed with lust and power, he violated her with a passion. Holding down her body, which thrashed its resistance like a pitiful creature caught in a trap, he entered the small crevice of her anus. The more she screamed, the more exhilaration coursed through his veins. By the time he'd finished, he was wonderfully exhausted. She could not move, as the pain racked her body.

Her tears fell on to the pillow, and her sobs were a muffled but audible sound. He didn't care. What was all the fuss about? He'd done it to so many, who'd been more than grateful. Trust her to be different, the prissy bitch.

CHAPTER NINE

Morgan sat in the church of St. Patrick. It was the only place that made her feel whole again. It brought back memories of her happy childhood years and all the things that had been sacred to her. Their warmth comforted her agonised mind. The teachings and the hope of her Catholic upbringing would show her the way, she was sure.

'Bless me, Father, for I have sinned. It is has been two months since my last confession.'

How was she to start her confession? *Where* was she to start? Perhaps with the things that were in the forefront of her mind.

'I want a divorce.'

'Why is that, my child?'

How should she justify her need to be free? Tactfully, she told the good priest the nature of the violation she had suffered from her husband. Surely he would see why she needed a divorce. But once a Catholic, always a Catholic.

'You must think of the great martyrs and their suffering,' the priest told her gently. 'You must ask God to help you. Pray for your husband, for he is in need of your prayers, not your desertion. In the eyes of God, you are and always will be married. Pray and you will be given the strength.'

Morgan continued her confession. 'I have held thoughts about another man. I have a longing to be loved by him. I can't get him out of my mind. I feel dirty and sordid. Soon there will be nothing left of me, Father. How long can I go on? I don't know who I am any more, or where I belong. I feel so alone.'

Her tears flowed as she recited her penance. Purgatory was, to her, the life she was living now. Was this how her devotion to Conran was to be repaid? Her love had died, yet for the rest of her days, she would be saddled with the man who had defiled her. What life was there left? It would be impossible to go back, to live with the horrifying memory of last night. And if it happened again? The thought struck terror in her heart.

Morgan left the church of St Patrick, feeling let down by the church and her religion. It had not protected her as she thought it would.

He'd risen early, still high from the coke he'd snorted the previous night. Just a little more for breakfast and he'd be fine. He'd be buzzing to fuck. God, it made him feel good! Life glowed on this gear. Everything was a buzz most of the time, until… For paranoia was one of the less desirable side-effects of cocaine and amphetamines. Lately, he'd been doing too much and a paranoid psychosis had started to creep in slowly. He'd fought his sensibilities at first, pushing the outrageous thoughts from his mind. No, people were not looking at him in a knowing fashion. How could they know his secrets? They were just people in the street. Yet as he turned a corner, he often looked twice just to check no one was following him. He kept Gregory Scott close by him at all times, never going to the car alone. He even took Scott with him when he visited his mistresses.

How he thrilled these women! How honoured they were when he let them suck his cock. Of course, the truth of it was: they feared him. They dreaded his visits, hated the musty store room in the casino where he frequently took the current objects of his lust. Most of them loathed his touch, but who dared say no? They would have to show great pleasure at his laboured lovemaking that would go on and on, due to his continual snorting of cocaine. Sure, there was the odd one who thought herself something special and bragged about the attention the boss had bestowed on her, even to the point of taking liberties at work. Hilary dealt with these misplaced females. They never stayed for long afterwards. Down the road they went, tail between their legs.

Morgan walked the streets, not caring where she was going; just walking. She couldn't face going home. As if by accident, she found herself on the housing estate where Hilary lived. Recognising her whereabouts, Morgan knocked on the door. Perhaps she had subconsciously headed for her friend's house.

With tea brewed and biscuits laid on the plate, they sat in the kitchen.

'I envy you, Hilary, you know.'

'Can't think why. Surely you have everything?'

'No, not really.'

'Come on, what's wrong? Last night was a huge success. You should be delighted.'

'Yea, sure...' There was a pregnant pause. 'You know, I'd give anything to live in a house like this, with a family, simplicity.'

Was the bitch patronising her? No, she probably would settle for this.

'Oh H, tell me what to do, I'm so lost! I hate myself for my own thoughts. How can I love someone so strongly one minute, and then feel nothing but contempt the next?'

'You're talking about Conran, right? Oh, love, we all feel like that sometimes. Sometimes people hurt us without knowing it.'

'And when they hurt us intentionally?'

'Well, my love, we're all guilty of that sometimes.'

'Hilary, you're not stupid, you saw me last night. You're probably closer to me than anyone. You must have felt the electricity between Justin and me. And yes, I did flirt with him. God forgive me, but I felt so alive for the first time since Stewart died. I feel so guilty.'

'Stop being pathetic. Bloody hell, you Catholics! It proves you're human. Accept the fact that you aren't the Virgin Mary after all. You got married up the duff, for God's sake!'

'You make it sound so easy to live with, so boxed and clean.'

'Grow up, darling.'

And with those few simple words, Hilary gave her a little strength to go back into the lion's den.

CHAPTER TEN

For Morgan, the two years that passed seemed just moments dotted in time, spent counting the months that made up the frail female cycle. Yet each month brought no joy of maternity. Without the joy of a child to sustain her, Morgan felt she now had no stake in a marriage that was, for her, loveless. Lord know, she'd tried to cure her loathing for Conran Blake. A child would have been something to focus on, something to build on, a chance to put the wrongs right.

As for Conran, he still loved her, needed her, wanted her so badly. His mind loved her, his body loved her and his heart loved her, despite what he classed as his childish dalliances. Sure, he had the odd liaison, but what man would deny himself the pleasures of the female flesh when they were so readily available.

Morgan had asked him to take the test, a sperm count, just to check. His blunt refusal ended any further talk on the subject. After all, it couldn't possibly be his fault. They would just have to be patient. Anyway, he was far too busy, as the business was expanding on a grand scale. There was a new casino opening in London and he would be away for the best part of three months. No time to talk of babies now.

At first it was a novelty, having the house to herself, especially the bed and whole nights of undisturbed sleep. Although she missed Hilary, who had accompanied Conran to help interview the new staff, she didn't miss her husband's incessant sexual attentions. The days were long, sunny and relaxing, and she had begun to spend a lot of time at a new health club, meeting new friends and reviving her old zest for life.

It was here that she bumped into Justin, as if by the twisted hand of fate. She had enrolled on a first aid course the club was offering, and she instantly recognised the instructor. As if greeting an old friend, she enthusiastically shook his hand.

'Justin! You worked for my husband, right?'

'Briefly,' came back the curt reply.

'What are you doing here? I heard you'd been made casino manager at another branch.'

Of course, this information had come from Hilary, some weeks after the opening night saga. Justin had not been sacked, Hilary had assured her, just employed elsewhere. Morgan, relieved that no damage had been done, had thought no more of it.

'No, I work here now and I'd like to keep this job, so if you could just let me get on with it. Or do you intend to have me fired from here too?'

'Wait, what are you talking about? I had nothing to do with it!'

'Forget it, it doesn't matter now.'

'No, please, I need to talk with you.'

'It was a dirty trick, Mrs Blake, but now it's past, so if I could just get on with my job.'

'Justin, please let me explain. I tried... I mean I didn't lead you on purposely, I just wasn't thinking. Give me a chance to make up with you.'

'What am I supposed to think? Your husband didn't mince his words. And then, to add insult to injury, they said I'd taken a bribe from a punter!'

Morgan felt sick with anger. Okay, she expected as much from Conran, but why had Hilary lied to her? Perhaps she didn't know the truth.

Suddenly she leaned against the wall, feeling faint. In spite of himself, Justin was concerned. 'Hey, Mrs Blake, are you all right?'

Quickly, she recovered her composure and stood strong. This was a waste of time, she could never prove to him that she knew nothing about his sacking.

'Look, Justin, you can choose not to believe me, the privilege is yours and if it makes things any easier, I'll even give up the course. I have no intention of disturbing you or causing any trouble in your life. In fact, I'll leave right now and you can get on.'

With that she grabbed her bag and headed for the door. She was halfway down the corridor before she heard him call, 'Wait, wait!'

No, she'd prove to him how sincere she was. She chose to ignore the calls.

'Wait, for God's sake, lady, just a bloody minute!'

This did have the desired effect in a round about way.

'And who do you think you're talking to, might I ask?'

'It was the only way I could get your attention. God, you're stubborn!'

'No, I'm just determined to make you believe me.'

'It worked, believe me, beyond a shadow of a doubt.'

To Morgan, first aid proved akin to brain surgery. Still, she scraped through her first certificate, helped by Justin, who was becoming a firm friend.

Her performance on the running track was something else. She competed against other clubs, nothing major, just locally, but it gave her a new-found confidence and focus. It was nice to see Justin standing on the edge of the track, should anybody fall or twist an ankle. He encouraged her, pushed her on. After each performance, they'd discuss the competition over a drink in the club. Morgan enjoyed the freedom, the normality of her new life. Even her longing for a child had eased, and the pain of her loss had mellowed if not vanished.

On this particular day, Justin brought over drinks and sandwiches.

'You know,' Morgan told him, 'you've never gone into detail about what happened that day at the casino.'

'No, well, it's past.'

'I want to know.'

'Ask your husband or Mrs Nugent.'

'No, I'm asking you.'

'Look, Morgan, I don't know what's going on down there, and to be quite frank, I don't want to know.'

'What do you mean, Justin?'

'He's your husband. It's up to you to ask him.'

In her turn, she'd never told Justin much about her marriage, it was all far to humiliating to have to admit you'd made a mistake and married a monster. After all, there was fun to be had at the club, good times. Conran would be home too soon. Why spoil things with talk of her marriage?

'Conran tells me nothing. To be honest, I don't ask. Why should I? The business never interested me, finance isn't my cup of tea. As for the casino, well, I used to work there, but when I married Conran I wanted a family.'

Justin could not believe the naivete of this woman. She really had no idea. Not that he was an authority, but he did know things weren't as they should be. They never were in the gambling industry. But certain things spoke for themselves. Take the evening he'd been sacked, for example...

Justin had chipped up as usual, the roulette wheel was ready as he waited for his next punters. Mrs Nugent was making her usual Gestapo-like inspection, until she came to his table.

'Office please, Mr Edwards, right now.'

Something told him that he wasn't exactly invited for afternoon tea. Well, he had been out of order over-stretching his break and dancing with the boss's wife. He deserved an earful, no doubt.

In the office, Conran Blake was feeling bad. The buzz from the morning had worn off and he was coming down with a bang. His mind refused to concentrate on any one thing and he felt irritable. He also looked rough, and he could hardly stop shaking His nostrils, now sore from snorting coke, meant that he could no longer take it nasally. An alternative was to insert it anally. A bit of a piss-off, but the feeling went straight to his loins and oh, the erection was bloody good! Couldn't concentrate though, must concentrate. What did he have to do? Oh yea, that was it, get rid of lover boy. How much did he know? How long had he been employed here? Better ask Hilary, she'd know. Was Edwards a special or a regular employee? Had he been on any jobs for the organisation? Fucking hell, he needed to know so that he could get things organised, decide whether to dispose of Edwards completely, or just get shot. If he was a special, then he'd need the men to terminate this minor irritant.

Hilary appeared in the nick of time to help sort things out, good old girl that she was.

'Hilary, look what's... Oh fuck, I'm not quite with it today. Could you...?'

'Here, allow me.'

Good old Hilary served her master with his much needed pick me up. She knew he'd feel better soon and his head would once again function properly. And so it was Conran Blake soon got himself back in the driving seat and performed at top level.

So, Edwards was just a regular employee who knew nothing of Blake's criminal goings on. Give the guy a bit of a hard time, set an example to the rest of the staff - they were all getting a little cocky lately. He'd seen the way they looked at him when he walked through the casino. Was there something going on? Were they planning something? Of course nothing was going on, this was his paranoia.

Justin was shown into the office by Hilary, who stood guard next to Scott. Conran sipped on a lemonade. Alcohol brought him down on the gear, so better to stay clear of it.

'Hilary, get Mr. Edwards's coat.'

Justin said nothing.

'Your employment ceases as of this minute.'

'Look, Mr. Blake, I know I was out of line extending my break, but just...'

Conran cut him dead. 'Oh, it's much more serious than that, Mr Edwards. Sexual harassment of the female staff. Sexual harassment of my wife, so she tells me. Also accepting bribes.

We cannot tolerate this kind of thing.'

Justin was dumbfounded. 'This is ridiculous! I haven't done any of this!'

Wendy was shown into the office, her face pumped up and her eye badly blacked.

'Are you sure it was Mr. Edwards?'

'Positive, Mr Blake. He came at me like an animal. I was so scared. I told him I had a boyfriend, but he didn't seem to care. He grabbed me and…'

'Ssh, it's okay, my dear. Hilary, take her out and get her a nice cup of tea.'

Wendy had, in fact, taken the blow from Scott. She had no choice. Scott had enjoyed himself, he hated women, they were all trouble. The odd smack did them good, brought them into line.

Act two. Enter a special employee.

'I'm afraid I witnessed Mr Edwards accepting bribes off two people last night, to the amount of £50 each.

'This is bloody outrageous!' stormed Justin. 'What the hell is going on here?'

'Goodbye, Mr Edwards.'

He was shown out of the casino in a daze. He had a mind to go right back in, or bring the gaming board into it. However, he hadn't the power to prove his innocence against Blake, and besides it would mean risking his dealer's licence. No, he could do nothing. Sure, he knew what the game was. Blake's wife had flirted with him to get her husband jealous, then blamed him for harassing her.. There was nothing he could do.

Whilst on board ship he'd taken courses in first aid, body contouring and various other pursuits to keep himself busy throughout the day. Maybe now was the time to try something different. Yea, maybe this was his chance for a new career. It had been just the push he needed to break free from the tables.

'Look Morgan,' he was telling her now, 'things aren't always as they seem. What the hell! All's well that ends well, eh?'

'No, it's wrong. How could Conran do this? I won't deny that we had words that night after we left the casino. Yes, I did flirt with you, and I'm sorry. But I never told him you'd harassed me! After we left, he told me he'd get rid of you. I begged him not to, told him it was my fault. In the end, he assured me you'd get to keep your job and nothing would be said. How stupid could I have been! No wonder you hated me!'

'Look it's in the past. Come on, forget it. I'll drive you home.'

As they drove, Morgan stared out of the window, not knowing what to think. Where had the girl with bruises come from? Perhaps they used make-up, or maybe… Oh hell, she didn't know what to think. Why hadn't Hilary told her, she must have known the truth? Why had Hilary gone along with Conran? Why did Conran have to be so brutal? Okay, so he wanted to fire Justin, but he could have done that without all the scenario. It was as if they wanted to humiliate him, play power games, even scare him out of the way.

'Penny for them,' smiled Justin. 'Come on, talk to me. You never really opened up to me. I don't want to pry, but it's just that you look sort of lost every now and again. One minute you're bouncing high speed along a track, giggling over milkshakes like a schoolgirl, and then something in you stops, as if you're remembering something.'

'I've always been a day dreamer.'

He didn't leave her at the front door, as he was accustomed to. Not this time. He went inside at her request. The smell of coffee filtered around the kitchen. Morgan fussed over the cups, her hand shaking a little. Was this it, was this the moment she knew would inevitably come? The moment she longed for, yet dreaded, the premeditated sin?

She turned to reach for the sugar. His arms found the small of her waist. He pulled her round to face him and they kissed. He led her by the hand into the living room and there they made love. Softly and slowly they made love, a love that soothed the soul and brought peace to both.

Conran stretched out a weary arm to reach for the light switch. Grunting, he fought to keep the light from this eyes. God, what time was it? Four-ish. He couldn't remember what the arrangements were. Was Scott picking him up, or was it Hilary? Or had he said he'd phone first? He stared at the immobile body by his side. Bella, Bella. You could say that again! She was good, bloody good. The way she'd handled his cock, throwing back the sperm into that sensuous little mouth of hers, rolling the hot liquid on her tongue first. Not bad for a nineteen-year-old. Yes, he would keep this little miss's number for future reference.

Hilary arrived to pick him up, bringing a clean shirt and other necessaries. She ran the shower to warm it up for him, then made coffee. As he enjoyed the water cleansing him of the smell of sex, Hilary went to remove the baggage in the bed.

'Party's over, kid. Go and play in the school yard.'

'Who the fuck do you think you are?'

Hilary grabbed a fist of hair and threw the naked Bella into the hall, followed by her clothes. Just as she was about to shut the door on the girl, Conran came to see what all the commotion was about.

'Hilary, that's enough! Bella, get back into bed.'

Bella smiled a smile of triumph.

'Get the girl a coffee. Now!'

Conran scrambled into his trousers and left the room, leaving instructions for Bella to contact him later in the week. She was about to start a new career as a croupier.

Before leaving, Hilary accidentally poured steaming hot coffee over little Miss's face. That would delay her career a bit! All these bitches wanted Peter... no, she meant Conran... or was it Peter? Well, she was tired.

Over the house hung a silence that had not been noticeable before, a sort of anticipation. Or perhaps it was dread. Maybe even the house noticed that something was in the air, an aura of change. Morgan had not phoned Justin that morning. What was the point? It was over. Much as they both wanted it, there was no possibility of a future together.

She loved him, of that there was no doubt. But reality had to be considered. Justin had agreed to her wishes, despite the pain that had rendered him inconsolable, a hurt that tore through his heart like a knife. How was he going to get through the days? How would he survive the nights alone? Their love had been short-lived, nothing more than a glimpse of something special. Was he right to walk away and leave her with that animal? After all, it was apparent that Morgan had no real understanding of the extent of her husband's criminality. She had said no to their love, and he must respect her decision. She had married Conran for better or worse.

Conran came home burdened with gifts for the woman he loved. Yes, he did love her. On seeing the sleek yet curvaceous figure of his wife standing at the front door, he felt glad to be home. The September breeze blew the long blonde hair gently across her face. She looked young and radiant. In fact, he thought she looked a little different somehow, but he was not quite sure how.

That night Morgan performed for her husband the ritual of love. Conran still enjoyed the feel of his wife's body, her essential purity. Sex with Morgan was so unlike the whoreish, dirty fucking Bella had provided. Still, there was a time and a place for everything, and at this time he liked to be with his clean-living, wholesome wife.

As her husband took his pleasure, Morgan thought of no one except Justin, her mind and body longing for him. The crudity of her husband's touch repelled the blood in her veins. How was she to live her life in the arms of a man she despised? Yet she had no choice.

Morning came, bringing Hilary round to the house to pick up Conran. It was time to see how things were at Billings Casino. Had the mice been playing while the cat had been away?

Conran was expecting a new consignment to be delivered, which he would have to test for quality - ensure that the amphetamine had not already been cut and that the coke was good. He might have a little dab himself, as he was feeling tired. Just a dab to pep himself up, not forgetting that he had made himself a promise to cut down. A little dab would do no harm.

They arrived at the office. His first instruction was to Hilary: she should call the florists and order his wife a dozen red roses. This Hilary did, with a bitter taste in her mouth. So the Irish whore was back in favour! Her hopes for intimacy in London had been dashed, as Bella had seen to Conran's needs. Bitch! So when was he going to make time for her?

She edged closer to him as he sat at his desk. 'Conran. It's been a long time. Have you forgotten how good we are together?'

Conran looked into the face of the woman who so reminded him of his mother. It made him laugh to think that this ageing slut had once so stirred his desire. God, did she really think it had been her who had turned him on? Hadn't she understood that it was the fantasy, not the tart?

'Run along, Hilary. I'm busy, there's a good little foot soldier.'

'Surely we can meet soon and...'

He sneered at her. 'My dearest, Hilary, why should I want to fuck that overused body of yours, when I have a wife who looks and smells as fresh as the day? Do run along now, and I might let you give me a blow job later if you're a very good girl.'

The humiliation tortured her, the betrayal ripped through her like a knife. What was she now? Nothing more than an employee. A good little foot soldier, a good little girl indeed! This was not happening. He had not said those things to her. Peter loved her, wanted her, he hadn't been unkind to her, he hadn't suggested she was getting old, was no longer desirable.

Once home, Hilary sought the comfort of sleep, sweet sleep. Once asleep all would be well. There would be no more pain.

Damn, no pills! The memory of the interview with Conran flashed through her head. Reaching for a kitchen knife, she cut deep into the flesh of her breast, again and again until the blood ran freely, soothing her hurt. The wound gaped and bled, offering an outlet for her degradation.

The cutting went on for some days, draining her of energy and colour. She began to look like a zombie, eyes black and staring. She did not eat or drink. Cutting into her own flesh released the humiliation inside her soul, and she gouged herself where it would not show to the world: the inside of her thighs, her breasts, her stomach, until it all seeped out - the poison she believed had invaded her veins.

Morgan spent the days trying to keep busy: shopping, reading, anything to escape the torment of her own mind. In moments of madness she would see his face, feel the warmth of his touch and the gentleness of his voice would echo like a love song in her head. For a brief moment she would lapse and indulge in her fantasies, before reality beckoned again.

The shop was full. As she touched the gentle fabric of a cotton shirt, her mind began to drift. Conran always wore silk; Justin wore cotton. There was something so warm and dependable about cotton...

It went dark then light as the hand that had covered her eyes was removed. She turned to see Justin holding up his hands.

'Oh God! What are you doing here?'

'I saw you come into the shop and I couldn't let the opportunity pass. Morgan…'

'Justin, someone could see us!'

'Just a coffee. Come on, we can get one on the fourth floor. Don't ask me to walk away,, Morgan, not yet.'

There was so much to say, and yet they needed no words. Feeling the warmth of each other as their bodies gently touched was enough. He looked into her face and saw the sadness there. Tears welled up from deep within her, and he gently kissed them away, not caring who might see. A couple of young girls at the next table giggled at such a show of affection.

The encounter was over all too soon, the memory to be put away in a box and savoured for the grim days and nights ahead.

October brought rain and hail. The winds were cold as the nights drew in. Morgan drove through the crowded streets at rush hour. She should have booked an earlier appointment, but what the hell, what did she have to rush for? An hour in the car was an hour less spent in that prison of a house - an hour to indulge in her fantasies.

Pulling up outside the Medical Centre, she recognised the car alongside hers. Hilary! Shit! What was *she* doing here? My God! There was no getting away from Conran and his bloody employees. The relationship between Morgan and Hilary had been strained lately. Morgan felt she could no longer trust or communicate with the woman, so she had avoided her.

Each feigned pleasure at the chance meeting, though Morgan was shocked at Hilary's gaunt appearance.

'Morgan! Conran didn't tell me you were ill.'

'No, well, it's nothing really. I just need a tonic. You?

'Sleeping pills.'

'Really, Hilary? I didn't know you had trouble sleeping.' The tone of sarcasm was noticeable. Hilary left, clutching her prescription. It was just as she got into the car that an idea struck home. She waited in the car park.

When Morgan came out, she drove through the rain as it lashed angrily against the windows. She didn't know how or where she was driving. The shock had left her stunned, scared yet enlightened. She was going to have Justin's child. There could be no doubt about it, when she calculated the dates. She had conceived in the middle of August. Conran had returned home during the last week in September, and it was now into the third week of October. For nearly three months a child had been growing inside her, and she hadn't for a moment suspected. She had simply put her missed period down to nerves and upset.

What to do now? Hell! What was she going to do? She had no one to turn to for advice. There was a chance that she could pretend the baby was her husband's. There were ways. Yet the thought of allowing Conran to touch the child, the child Justin and she had made from love, horrified her.

As she looked in her rear mirror, she thought that the car following behind was getting too close, but it was raining so hard and the night was so black that she could not make out the colour or make of the vehicle. Damn the bloody driver! Close wasn't the word for it: she was almost being trailed. God, was there nowhere she could be alone to think? She pulled over, allowing the car to overtake. But it didn't; it pulled over too. Morgan began to feel nervous so she hit the accelerator hard and surged ahead. The car behind did likewise, only faster, as it veered into the side of her and pranged her off the road.

Hilary hadn't planned to do it like this, but hey, it was time the bitch was put out of the way for good, then Conran would find time for her. She had lain in wait for the Irish whore to leave the clinic, planning to follow her back to the house. But it hadn't quite worked out like that. Where was the bitch going anyway, driving into the night like a madwoman?

Morgan's car had skidded down the bank and into a tree. Her head hit hard against the horn in the steering wheel and Hilary, pleased with her work, drove away at speed.

Morgan must have been unconscious for a couple of hours, for the next thing she knew she was in hospital, Conran at her side. Slowly she came round, startled.

'Darling, you've had an accident,' he said, all loving concern.

'No, Conran, no accident. Someone was trying to run me off the road, maybe to kill me.'

'Don't be silly, darling. Who would want to kill you?'

'Someone ran me off the road,' she said firmly.

Then she remembered the baby. 'My God! My baby!'

Conran recognised the look of horror on her face. 'It's okay. Our child is safe. Why didn't you tell me before? Oh, I know you. You wanted to be sure. I'm so happy, darling - this is our second chance.'

He left so that she could get some sleep. But the turmoil of her thoughts made her head pound, almost to exploding point.

CHAPTER ELEVEN

Hilary was waiting in the room at the bottom of the house. Soon Peter would be here to share her joy - the joy of freedom, of knowing once more that he was safe. So she sat, waiting calmly. Soon he would come to her and partake of her again, like he had done so many times before. The port was ready, the room aired.

Conran arrived home, took a shower, and dressed ready for his evening at The Reading Rooms. It was a place of sombre tranquillity, a place to read the daily papers, enjoy a brandy and the company of successful, like-minded men of means and culture. Tonight would be his night, a night to share his joy at the prospect of being a father. Yes, a night spent with men of his class. This was not the time to be playing with whores and dirty bitches.

As he poured himself a coffee, he thought he heard a noise, as if someone was moving round the house. Once he had assured himself it was not coming from upstairs, he went into the bowels of the house. A muffled sound was coming from the smallest room. Conran took the key and slowly opened the door.

A bizarre sight met him. There stood Hilary, drinking whisky, her face painted in make-up that gave her the look of a deranged clown. In her own eyes, it made her look inviting. Well, it had worked for the Irish whore. Why couldn't it work for her? And was this not the same blue gown the whore had worn on the re-opening night of the casino? So, it was a little tight. It didn't matter; soon it would be discarded. Her lipstick had got a bit smudged from the drink; her eyeliner and face powder too. But those were minor details; it wasn't your face they were looking at. Didn't she look fine and dandy all dressed up? Yes, one could be sure to catch the male eye, looking as she did at this moment.

'Peter, come in. I knew you'd come sooner or later.' Taking Conran's hand, she smiled. 'Oh, I know you're scared, but really it's okay now, everything's going to be fine.'

The sight was nauseating. Her skin seemed to hang from her bones. The many open wounds on her body wept red-tinged pus.

'Hilary, what in hell's name are you doing?'

'Oh I know what you like. I know what they all like from a woman.'

She started to massage her breasts and dip her hand between her thighs.

'Lick me Conran, lick me like you used to lick me.'

Pulling open the gown she displayed the now rancid flesh that had not been allowed to heal in between mutilations. 'Look, my darling. I've punished myself for you. I bleed for you.' Inserting a finger deep within herself, she gave out a moan of pleasure. 'I've been really good. I got rid of the whore once and for all. I know how you hated her, how she tried to abuse you, how she used you. I've stopped her. We won't be parted again.'

Words that Morgan had spoken at the hospital came flooding back to him. *'Someone was trying to run me off the road, maybe to kill me.'*

'She's in the dirt where she belongs, crawling in the dirt. I've been waiting for the naughty boy to come home and he's late, so he's going to get a spanking, once and for all.'

'Hilary, what did you do to my wife?' Conran was speaking through gritted teeth. 'Hilary, what did you do to Morgan?'

Hilary suddenly became violent and started to scream like a wild banshee. 'Fucking Morgan, fucking Morgan! It's always fucking Morgan! Well, I got the bitch.'

Conran felt the flash across his head, felt the old familiar pain. 'You hurt my wife, Hilary?'

'You're dead fucking right I did.' She became calm again. 'Please, Peter.'

Conran's voice was dangerously quiet. 'Why do you keep calling me Peter? I've noticed it before.'

'I don't know what you're talking about. Come here, this is no time for talking.'

Undoing the dress, Hilary stood naked before him, her mutilated flesh a mass of festering wounds. He felt the pain inside his head as he took her by the throat and proceeded to beat her mercilessly. From one wall of the room, she bounced to the other, her head hitting the hard brick with a thud. Blood spattered the walls and the stone floor, then spurted from her mouth as she lay unmoving on the floor. Conran felt the frenzy work up inside his head, so once again, he used the old technique to calm himself. Taking up position beside the prostrate body on the floor, he sang gently, softly, as if to ward off the deadly rage that gripped him.

'Hush little baby don't say a word, Poppa's gonna buy you a mocking bird. And if that mocking bird don't sing, Poppa's gonna buy you a diamond ring.'

Then, reaching out, he took hold of a nearby poker and began to flay the helpless body lying at his feet. When he had finished, he took the twitching form and held it across his lap, holding the head to his breast. He began to sing to the woman who had been a mother and a lover to him, singing as she released her last tortured breaths. Then Conran dropped her to the floor, left the room and locked the door behind him.

The eyes slowly opened, as blood poured into them. A hand, red with gore, forced one finger to use the thick red liquid as ink to form the words 'Irish Whore' on the cold stone floor.

Morgan was discharged from the hospital two days later, fit and well though still a little traumatised by her ordeal. Conran was glad to have his wife home. Now that she was pregnant again, he would make sure she was looked after. Nothing was going to get in the way of his second chance to have a son.

Morgan could do nothing but pretend to share his joy in the forthcoming child - his child, as he believed. Now the true identity of the baby's father would remain a secret for the rest of her life. It was for her and her conscience to live with. Thankfully, the doctors had not told Conran how far gone she was. They must have taken it for granted that he already knew.

Six months into the pregnancy, Morgan began to prepare for the arrival of her new hope, her new existence. She had decided to have a good look around in the cellars. Perhaps the basement could be made into a nursery or playroom. The whole floor could be re-decorated and opened up.

Morgan found a door heavily padlocked, just at the bottom of the dark corridor. It didn't take much to lever the door open, just enough so she could see inside. It was dark and smelt musty. Still, it was worth having a proper look, she could always have it air-conditioned. With a crowbar and a little bit of muscle, the padlock fell to the ground.

The stench was the first thing that hit her as she opened the door in the dark. There must be a light switch, for God's sake. Apparently not!Hell, she thought, when was this room last opened? Not since his mother had been alive, by the smell of things. It was beyond dark, almost deathly, as she slowly made her way inside. Feeling for the walls, she took each step slowly. There was an old fireplace against the wall that still contained dust and ashes from God knew how long ago. A half-empty bottle stood on the fireplace, she took a sniff. Port! Funny, not that old by the smell of it. A discarded cigarette butt or two sat by the half empty bottle. But where was the smell coming from? Her foot bumped against something solid on the hard floor. She looked down to see what was at her feet.

Horror struck her as she ran from the room and up the stairs to the first floor and into the living room. There she knocked back a stiff shot of vodka. Calm, calm, she must be calm. Perhaps it had been a trick of the dark - it could have been anything, the light had been bad.

'Get a bloody grip,' she said aloud to herself, 'you've got to go back, you've got to check.' The second time she went back armed with a flashlight and candles.

Slowly, cautiously, she entered again. Moving across to the fireplace, forcing herself, she took the few steps to where she thought she had felt the body at her feet. The flashlight gave off sufficient brightness now and she could see into the dark. There it was, the thing she had bumped into. She knelt down to be sure. Indeed it was a body. Her hand flew to her face to ward off the stench, her eyes wanting to turn away, her legs wanting to run. But she couldn't. The fingers seemed to be pointing at something. The words 'Irish Whore' had dried in the blood on the stone floor. And there was something else, more words: 'Stewart,' it read. 'Stewart, Irish bastard, die…'

The flashlight smashed to the floor as Morgan fled up the stairs and into her own bedroom. Grabbing a bag, she stuffed what clothes she had to hand into it, and fled out of the house into the car. Ireland, Ireland! She would go home. There she would be away from whatever was going on in the house. Whatever Conran was doing, she would be away from it all and safe. In Ireland she would not be found. Oh, he might look for her in Dublin but not in Achill. He would never find her there. After all, she had never told him about the truth about her childhood home. Perhaps this was why. Could it be that she had always felt some strange intuition warning her of the future? No time to think, must get away, get away. Home, home to Uncle Robert and the house she was born in. Yes, there she would have her child. In Ireland, and on Achill soil she would bring this innocent child into the world, before Conran's filth and degradation could mar the child forever.

The wind screamed around the old farmhouse, as if it too felt the pain of childbirth. The sea crashed against the shore as the elements welcomed the new-born of Achill. The night seemed longer and the darkness darker. In the room that had been her mother's, and screaming in agony, Morgan pushed into the world Mary Jane Blake. The child arrived weighing 6lbs and 5oz, and blessed with a mass of black hair.

The freshness of June restored light and sunshine to the land, as Morgan gazed out onto the Atlantic coastline that ran along the shores of Achill. The smell of burning turf fires filtered through the air, so familiar, so reminiscent of her childhood. It took her back to the days of the great barn dances. Bringing in the turf had been fun - or was she simply sweetening up the memories, the only simple innocent memories she had left? The simple lifestyles of Achill people, the people themselves, were the only memories she could bear to look back on.

Her father, a strong man, a big man, and a learned one at that, had related tales of her ancestry on many an occasion when it was too cold and dark to go out. By the fireside he told his tales and stories. Many an Achill father or grandfather had been in De Valera's Army, and on occasion, the British soldiers, believing there were a guns hidden in the houses of Achill folk, had searched each dwelling from top to bottom. Once they'd torn up the floorboards and pulled homes apart, stone by stone, while her own mother, no more than a child then, continued to shovel the turf in the nearby lean-to.

With the help of her Uncle Robert, Morgan would pass these tales on to Mary Jane, her future now, the core of her existence.

The brightness of the sun and the freshness of the wind soon restored Morgan to true health. Life in Achill was peaceful, the land suited her and her child, now two months old. Learning to relax and not to be continually looking over her shoulder, Morgan Blake started to shake off the past and breathe afresh hope for the future.

Conran had searched high and low, leaving no stone unturned. From coast to coast of the British mainland he had sent his people to look for his wife. A score of people had gone to Ireland and searched in Dublin. No trace could he find, nothing led to nothing. He cursed himself for his negligence, for not moving the fucking bitch's body. Oh yes, in death Hilary had had the last laugh.

The club! Why had he not thought of it sooner? That bloody club, where she had spent so much of her time while he was away. His wife must have had a friend, someone would know. Maybe someone was hiding her and my God, if they were… Mustn't rush straight on in. Send someone undercover; as a new client. The girl didn't argue. Any attractive female member of the team would do.

Playing her part well, taking her time, the girl befriended one of the trainers and first aid teachers. Justin was a lamb to the slaughter. After a sexual encounter, in the afterglow of physical affection, Justin talked of the sorrow he carried deep in his heart and of the great love he'd once had, now lost forever. He vowed he could never truly love again. The girl was all ears and sympathy.

She had done well and her bonus was stupendous. Gregory Scott sliced the head off Justin Edwards as easily as he would a hard boiled egg. The rest of the body he placed in a plastic bag and threw it in the river.

Conran vowed to find the whereabouts of his wife. He was wretched when the pain came, oh, so much more often, as he thought about the cruel betrayal he had suffered. How could she have done this? His own pure Irish rose had been nothing more than a whore. He had been fooled, deceived by his own love and heart.

Must not think any more, must try to sleep. Bella. Bella would mop his brow and wipe away the pain and the sweat. Dear Bella would ease his head when it felt as if it was going to explode. Calling her, she came running into the bedroom to see what else the spoilt bastard wanted of her. Fucking hell, she was pissed off with this, they never went out any more. Damn him, he wouldn't even go to the casino. He was dirty and unshaven. Hell, he couldn't even get it up any more. His call of 'Bella, Bella' was starting to sound like 'nurse, nurse'. Then there was the constant crying out of that bitch's name in the night. Fuck, no wonder she had left him. The stupid bastard had even tried to get her pregnant. Fuck you, she thought, as she swallowed her contraceptive in the bathroom where he couldn't see it. Was this right? Was it? At the age of nineteen having to frigg yourself off for kicks. The thought of leaving was a joy, but she liked the use of her legs too much. God, she'd happily find the bitch herself, if it meant being free from this prick.

She turned on the TV set, more out of boredom than anything else. He had just suffered another attack of his 'heads', as he called them. With the help of painkillers and a lullaby, the baby had gone to sleep. How she hated that, having to gently sing lullabies to him. She felt bloody silly, but it seemed to work and besides, it was worth having him out of her hair for a few hours. Stuffing crisps into her mouth, she sat back to watch. Bella decided to suffer the news before the film. Ireland, ha, wasn't that where the bitch was from? What a dickhead, would you believe it, some guy had crossed Europe and America only to land up in the middle of the night in the arse end of beyond, in fucking Ireland. Some arse end town at that. The news guy stood in the rain, as he showed the very place the idiot had landed some hours earlier.

Locals packed round the camera hoping to tell their story about how they had piled out of the pub to help pull the guy ashore. The camera man approached a woman holding a baby in her arms. Obviously she did not want to know as she turned away quickly. She was one hell of a good-looking woman, thought Bella, beautiful blonde hair, tall and skinny. Almost spitting the food out of her mouth, Bella shouted for Conran. Could it be? Well, fuck, Ireland wasn't such a big place was it? Yes, she'd seen the photos. God, he'd shown her his family photos a hundred times, so many times, before he'd cried into the night,

'Conran, for fuck's sake, I think I've found your wife.'

The news item went nationwide. Only those with any interest caught sight of Morgan and her child, as she turned from the eyes of the camera, and ran like a frightened child.

Bella had packed up and left the house once she was sure he was aboard the flight to Knock airport. From Knock he would travel by car to Achill Island. In a matter of a few hours he would be reunited with his love for just a short time. For a time, until the moment came to say goodbye.

CHAPTER 12

Morgan thanked old Cornelious for the delivery of the newspapers and shut the gate behind him. Sifting through them, she stopped to check if Robert's English Express had been delivered, as it so often did not turn up. There it was, a day late as usual, but at least this time it had arrived.

Reading the front page, Morgan froze. The bodyless head of a man believed to be the missing Justin Edwards had been found in a boating lake. The police were trying to contact Conran Blake, owner of the Billings Casino, to help them with their enquiries, as it was believed that Blake had been a previous employer of Mr. Edwards. No contact as yet had been made with Blake, as the authorities had been informed by a close friend of his, a Miss Bella Longthorn, that the gentleman in question was currently in Ireland seeking a reconciliation with his estranged wife and child.

Morgan dropped the paper and ran inside the house. No time to explain to Uncle Robert. Just grab the child and get off the island. He could be here now, watching her every move.

Mary Jane sat quietly in her cot, listening to the wind that tinkled the charms hanging from the ceiling. Gurgling and smiling, the child was wrapped in a blanket and soon clutched to her mother's breast. Robert was shovelling the turf out back, unaware of his terror-stricken niece inside the house.

A darkness descended on Achill, as the clouds moved in on the freshness of the daylight hours. Cold air stiffened fast around the island. The sea conjured up its devils to torment the rocks and cliffs. A woman ran towards the small drawbridge that joined Achill to the mainland. The wind blew a torrent of rain into her face as the tempest roused itself. Close now, close to any chance there might be of escape, the bridge slowly raised into the sky and Achill was now indeed an island.

'Dear God, no please!'

She cried as the menacing figure of Gregory Scott emerged from the shadow of the nearby inn and she saw the cruelly smiling face of Conran's best man.

'Better run, Mrs Blake, while you can.'

'Where's Conran? Where is he?'

She yelled, but Scott simply smiled at the distressed figure. Into the hills she ran, carrying her child. Blake stepped out of Ted Lavell's Inn and watched as his wife became no more than an outline in the distance.

Morgan stood at the top of the Minaun cliffs looking down upon the landscape that became Achill, Ireland., holding her baby close to her breast, wanting to run on. Yet from this point, there was nowhere left to run. And what would have been the good in running when there was nowhere left to hide? No answers! No, not in the sea or the wind. Just the threatening noises of the wild Atlantic Ocean. Maybe she had known that sooner or later he would find her, no matter where she ran to, or how far.

Then a voice seemed to be singing with the wind. A lullaby floated through the air. Standing alone and spectral at the top of the cliff was Conran.

'The child is not yours, Conran.'

'Oh my darling, I know that. Don't you think I know that?'

'You didn't have to kill him, you bastard, you didn't have to kill him. Now you've come for me. Do you want the both of us? Conran, you can take me; if that's the price, then I'll pay. But please let my daughter live. Don't kill my baby, please.'

He sang softly, sweetly. '*Hush little baby, don't say a word. Poppa's going to buy you a mocking bird, and if that mocking bird don't sing…*'

Slowly, he walked towards her on the soft slippery grass as if in a trance.

'Conran, listen to me, please!'

He kept on walking. Morgan fell to her knees in the dirt and placed the child near a rock that would shield it from the wind that rushed around them. Facing him, her back now to the edge of the cliff, she saw a look in the eyes of Conran Blake, something more than pity, something further than sorrow. Emptiness. It was the look of a man who had lived, but was now void of any feeling for truth, love or reality. In his eyes there was no future and no past, nothing left. It seemed that he was looking at her for the first time, as if he had not known this woman, not shared a life with her.

How beautiful she was now, as the torrent of wind gusted through the long blonde hair. The redness of her cheeks bore the freshness of youth. Something else - the pain in his head had gone. It had left him, for the first time in years. His head felt at peace. No lingering anxious pain to throb and dominate him. In between the drops of rain that fell upon them, the salty air mingled with her tears and perhaps a few of his. Thunder roared and cursed the land and the day. Holding his wife's hands up to him, it seemed fitting. Her softness, her warmth comforted him. Her smell pleased his senses. Oh how the little lambs were meant to be protected from themselves, to be taken care of, kept out of danger, kept from sin! After all, hadn't his mother known all about sin? Wiping away the tears from her eyes, he held her close.

The ground was now sodden, the earth seemed to slip into running pools of mud. Morgan looked down on her child as Conran held her. She sank to her knees and he picked her up out of the dirt, raised her to her feet, not roughly, but firmly, almost protectively.

'Oh, my wife, my mind loves you, my body loves you and my soul loves you. You know my mother would have liked you. Yes, she would, I'm sure she would. Walk with me.'

Together they approached the edge of the cliff.

'Can you feel the wind? You can almost taste the ocean!'

From hell the rain lashed upon our world. Morgan, her foot too close to the edge, slipped, her body twisting as she hung onto his arm. He pulled her back onto the ground, but the land had become a river of mud from the spewing rain. Lightning struck bright and hard. There was a cracking sound as Morgan again slipped over the edge. Conran almost lost his balance yet he managed to gain a foothold, still clutching the small delicate hands. He pulled back, his grip firm now as he looked down upon his wife dangling from the cliff. Her eyes screamed fear, her face almost contorted as she screamed for her life.

All that stood between life and death for Morgan now was her husband's grip. The jagged rocks and crashing sea waited for her below. Her life was in his hands.

Tears fell upon his cheek for he loved her, truly, he loved his wife. He screamed: 'Oh God , Oh God, *no!*' as he released his grip and her to die. For Morgan the struggle was over. She felt no weight, no breath as the wind carried her body down the cliff and into the vast ocean beneath. The sea welcomed the sacrifice.

Soon the wind eased and the land became still. The sun peeked its head out from behind the last great ugly black cloud. The smell of the summer flowers sweetened the air. Cattle again moved about the island. A gentle slurping sound replaced the angry crash as the sea lapped the shore line.

Amid the elements, a human cry could be heard from the top of the Minaun cliffs. Mary Jane Blake, still wrapped in her wet blanket, begged for attention.

Part Two

WHEN THE LULLABY ENDS

CHAPTER 13

Mary Jayne Blake gazed across the landscape and felt nothing but hate and contempt at the sight of the sea and cliffs that surrounded her. Closing her eyes, she longed for life and company, for the day she would be free of Achill, Ireland and the sorrow of her birth. The gulls taunted her so much at times, she found herself screaming back to them, begging them to stop. Maybe they too felt the anguish that had been inside her all her young life; maybe they too hated the island. Yet here in this place of raging winds and gushing sea, Mary Jayne had found a sort of bond. Perhaps the spirit of her mother still lingered, waiting to be saved from the tragic accident that had taken her.

It was on occasions when the early evening glazed the once bright blue sky with turquoise shades of grey that Mary Jayne felt as if something or someone was watching over her.

Her dreams were of other places, countries and capitals, different towns. Out there was a life to be lived, people to meet, excitement and adventures to be had. To live amongst the crowd, to go unknown, dress in short skirts and dance nights away, wear lipstick, meet boys. Yes, even to live on the dangerous side of life. Anything would be better than the staid existence Achill Island had to offer..

Uncle Robert and the local community had given her all the love they could and more, yet the love of a mother and father had never been hers. Not knowing where you came from left a void; not knowing anything left a hole somewhere inside only parental affection could fill.

Her mother had been very beautiful: she had been told that on many an occasion. Yet if she pursued the speaker into revealing more, her questions went unanswered. She knew simply that Morgan Blake had died very young. There had been a terrible storm which led to an accident and her mother's body had been discovered some three miles along the coast, drowned. The sea had claimed Morgan Blake and it had been God's will. That was the little Mary Jayne had ever been told about her beautiful, ill-fated mother. As for her father, she simply did not have one. Whenever she raised the question of her father, Uncle Robert would simply mutter something unintelligible and then scold her.

'Is it not enough you have the love and adoration of the whole island? Is it not enough I love you like my own and praised the good lord for bringing you to me when he did? Tell me, child, does all this mean so little that you need to ask questions I don't have the answers to?'

Responses like this made her feel guilty and ungrateful, so on these occasions she had walked the Wheelan Road through the rough terrain and up to the cliffs to think and sometimes cry a little. Alone, she would sit and stare at the photograph of her dead mother for hours and hours on end.

CHAPTER 14

The woman at the sink gazed into soapy bubbly water as she dried the last of the dishes and smiled to herself, a contented smile. It was the smile one smiles when thinking of the young and the funny questions they ask - questions Mary Jayne Simpson no longer cared to ask about the mystery concerning her parents. For now, years later, the young girl was but a memory inside the woman's head, and her thoughts now lingered upon her own family, the children and husband she loved so very dearly.

So much had gone before this time of domestic bliss. There had been another Mary Jayne then - the solicitor employed by Darwen and Philips, the young ambitious colleen who had thrived amongst the legal brains of Liverpool, learned the language, learned the rules. She had even learned to speak with an English accent. Success had brought Andrew into her life, a good, kind man, a man to build her life around. And that was just what she had done. Two children later and her world was full of the things she had never known but had always longed for. Catherine now seven and David five complemented everything in her life.

Rubbing his eyes, Andrew Simpson groaned. Morning was not his time of day. He did not like mornings at all. Did climbing out of a warm bed ever get any easier? No, he thought not. One day he would persuade his wife to lie in late and take it easy for a while. Oh well! Might as well get up. Day off, but tell that to the kids. He put on his robe, one of those rather feminine, Chinese-type things he didn't like at all, but as his wife had bought it for him as a gift, he wore it to please her.

Mary Jayne had this ability to be terribly silly when it suited her. Boy, he loved that! There was no doubt his woman was most definitely all woman. To Andrew, she had all the attributes a female should have: the girl, the lover, the wife, the mother. He considered himself a very fortunate man indeed.

Sitting down at the table, Andrew watched his wife as she reached up to get a cup. God! he thought. What a sight to behold! He smiled to himself when he considered his catch. A guy like him from the concrete jungle scoring a gorgeous, witty, intelligent lady and making her Mrs Simpson! Life was good.

Yet it had not always been so. No, for Andrew there'd been times in his life when only sheer strength had brought him through. Courage and hope had also played their part because when things had been bad for Andrew, they really had gone very bad and only a man of character and strength could have survived.

Born in the rough Manchester neighbourhood of Skimsdale, Andrew and Johnny Simpson had lived hand to mouth, running wild, doing what they liked when they liked. Mrs Simpson was always too drunk to care about, or even be aware of, the well-being of her two fine sons.

Andrew was quiet; Johnny was everybody's friend. Andrew watched from the wings, whereas Johnny would be the centre of attention. Andrew was sensitive and had a sense of morality - or perhaps it was a simple urge to better himself and be out of this fleapit they called home. Johnny just did not think about things too long or too hard. No, for Johnny life was for living and that was what he did to the full.

Andrew worried about Johnny. If Johnny wasn't home on time he fretted, pacing the house, waiting for Johnny to come walking through the door, and hoping that it would be before their intoxicated mother returned. It was best to avoid Mrs Simpson when she was, 'in drink', as one might say. It had never been a pretty sight watching Mother trying to remover her tights as some dirt-soiled pervert waited to reap the rewards of two vodkas and a gin and tonic. Andrew had witnessed this scene many times and had done his best to shield Johnny from it. For every man that enjoyed Mrs Simpson, the routine would be the same. Andrew would listen into the early hours of the morning as Mrs Deloris Simpson cried herself into oblivion once again, unaware of the two young boys sleeping in the adjacent rooms.

Johnny was blonde, of medium build, with a smile that lit up his whole face and eyes that sparkled when he laughed. And Johnny laughed a lot. Johnny was the boy of the neighbourhood. Everyone loved him and watched out for this likeable, cheeky, young teenager. Johnny's natural talent was making people smile at his silly jokes and often-daft antics. His deeds were of a nature soft and kind. His heart held room for everyone, the old dollies on the street, the kids that played the days away, the mothers, the young women. Oh yes. Not forgetting them too. Johnny loved the girls and the girls loved him. Life was one big laugh - or so Johnny thought.

His naivety would be the death of him.

Andrew Simpson was different from his brother. He liked to study. He liked books and all things that he considered educated his mind, therefore improving his prospects in life. From a young age, Andrew liked to be organised: things should be just how they were made to be; a place for everything and everything in its place. Life was meant to be like that, he was sure. It couldn't be that everyone lived as he did. He knew things elsewhere looked nice, different. Hadn't he seen it himself, the other side of town?

Shevington. That was where he wanted to be; to live in one of the large Victorian houses that stood strong and tall, domineering, powerful. Houses so different from the tiny, cramped maisonette he had been brought up in. You instantly knew what type of people lived in houses like that. Doctors, dentists, lawyers lived in houses like that. There was one thing for sure: no doctors lived in the heart of the concrete jungle; it was not for them. One day he would have a house very much like the ones in Shevington. If he studied hard, if he did well, he would take Johnny away from the constant abuse their mother hurled at them. They would be free of her - one day. Once there, maybe Johnny would take to reading books, and perhaps go back to school. Andrew saw study as the key to it all.

At first Mrs Simpson had tried to give the boys a decent life - well, sort of. Mr Simpson had long since done a runner on the announcement of her second pregnancy. That was the type of guy he was, flighty. Mr Simpson liked them young, he liked them soft and rounded in all the right places. In fact Mrs Simpson had been all of these things earlier on in life, but childbirth had taken its toll. It had stolen Mrs Simpson's youth, her looks - and her man with them. So what had been the point in trying to regain her looks? All that was left now was the sound of babies screaming to be fed - not her cup of tea. The vodka drowned the sound. That was very much the life of Mrs Simpson, drowning out that which she could not face.

Andrew washed, Andrew cleaned and cooked. Andrew took care of things. So a dirty tea towel or odd sock could often be found caught between the pages of the many books Andrew borrowed from the school library. How many times had he tried to get his younger brother to read? God knows, but Johnny had been more inclined to go out and have fun. The two children were so very different.

Now a father of two, Andrew had finally achieved his dreams: not Shevington but Port Sunlight, a safe place to raise his children, a community of fine upstanding, law-abiding citizens. Hey, this place even had its own art gallery, museum, theatre and bowling Greens, not one but two, right in the middle of the village. You would have been forgiven for thinking this was some remote country village due to the old-fashioned porched houses, each one slightly different in design and surrounded by flowers, a vast array of sunshine colours.

Port Sunlight was a beautiful place to live for now. The day would come when he would take his family and leave Liverpool forever. Johnny would have loved it, sure he would. Perhaps if Johnny had been given a decent start in life, a chance... Oh well, no point in thinking about what could have been, might have been. Things had worked out in the end for Andrew. He'd become successful. He had done it for himself and done it for Johnny. Johnny, hell, he missed Johnny! He'd never get over Johnny.

Closing the cupboard door, Mary Jayne Blake leaned against the oak fittings that ran all the way around the kitchen. Turning around, she looked at her husband. *Husband.* She wanted to say the word out loud but was far too shy. How handsome he was: tall, dark and handsome, perhaps even a little mysterious.

Feeling his body awaken, he pulled her close and reached inside her gown. The warmth of her flesh comforted him, eased him. Such softness to wrap himself around, to be close to, to love! Her aroma, her perfume aroused his desire as he thought of taking her there and then. He was all passion now and his body begged to be joined with hers. Now, *now* he needed to be inside her, his wife, his love, his woman. Mary Jayne, a little shocked yet flattered, could not refuse her husband's advances. She permitted his hardness to seek her womanhood.

Just then a beeping sound rudely interrupted the romantic moment.

'Damn!' Andrew swore, pushing back his thick, dark hair that had fallen into his eyes. It often happened like this. The job called, and he must do its bidding. Such was the lot of a Chief Inspector in the CID. Mary Jayne was understanding and supportive, as was her nature.

'Hey, come on honey, you know the score.'

'I know, I know. I'll get some clothes on.'

The car pulled away to the sound of screeching tyres. Not like Andrew, she thought, to drive so recklessly. Must be the case he was working on. Pressure to procure a result, that's what it was.

CHAPTER 15

Gazing into the long mahogany mirror, Mary Jayne took stock of her physiognomy. If you looked closely you could perhaps catch a glimpse of an Irish colleen, but Mary Jayne's looks truly belonged to an Egyptian princess. Long black hair lay softly on her shoulders; hair that was wild with curls. Her eyes were dark, darker than brown; it was the way they danced with vitality that made their gaze so alluring. With her gently sun-kissed skin, one might have thought her from an exotic foreign land. Mary Jayne was slim but not frail; delicate, evenly proportioned from head to foot, with legs contoured to slender perfection and a waist neatly nipped in. Her neck and shoulders were elegance itself, the curves of her breast almost sculptured. Indeed, Mary Jayne was naturally stunning.

Conran Blake shot the last dregs of his hot spunk far, far back into the throat of the girl who had been sucking his dick for the past five minutes. The hot liquid that gushed from his cock came forth so quickly it caused his body to jerk forward, making the girl gag. Deep, guttural sounds escaped from her involuntarily. Fuck, she thought, was that supposed to happen? Did everyone do that? Choke? 'Cause if that was it, the big *it*, the shag all the girls in her class went on about, then she'd rather go out and get pissed instead. Sex was horrid and she wanted no more of it. In fact she felt sick, very, very sick.

Conran took hold of his shrunken penis and placed it inside his trousers. Adjusting himself slightly over to the right, he zipped up his slacks. The girl got the hell out of it - on Conran's orders, of course. He couldn't help thinking virgins weren't what they used to be. Weren't they supposed to bleed a little? Or perhaps he'd forgotten. There weren't many around anyway. Glass collectors always came in handy. Good-looking, busy little workers could always find underpaid employment at Billings Casino - with extras thrown in.

Brushing back his hair, Conran Blake had no real objection to the guy in the mirror. Still blessed with the looks of the aristocracy, a tall, and still very handsome blond man stared back at him. Though he was now a little grey at the temples, Conran liked this distinguished air. He had taken care of his appearance for the most part of his life. Well, some time ago he had allowed things to get the better of him but now he was back on top form. Wiggling his moustache, he admired himself. Yes, he still had it. The blue eyes still sparkled and twinkled. His form was tall, broad, lean of the waist, a manly form. Blake had the kind of looks that would appeal to all women, no matter what their age. He had been blessed with his mother's genes. The years had been kind to him, in that sense.

Now, sitting at his desk, he began to shuffle his papers around. The papers told him that Blake Enterprises were performing very well, very well indeed. All the three casinos were raking it in, the hotels and restaurants were providing tasty profits. As ever, his non-tax related businesses allowed him that extra chunk of cash to fund his operation and act mainly as fronts.

Yes, the legal investments were a good cover for his narcotic operations and his hostess/ escort franchises. Oh yes! Mr Blake was doing very well indeed. Papers! What did paperwork mean? A whole lotta nothing. A whole lot of fucking around to keep the tax man happy. How much had he made over the years? he wondered. How much since way back, when he had opened his first casino? So many years had passed; so many things had happened.

Conran began to look back, to go back inside his memory. No! No! He must not go there, to that place. The cliffs, the Minuan cliffs. That time! That moment! He couldn't stop. He tried, tried but couldn't stop himself. Her face! Her cold wet face. The eyes so afraid, so much fear... Oh God! The fear, he had felt her fear. Had not the elements of the storm been so loud, he would have heard it too. Heard her breathe with what little breath she had, 'No please don't let me die!'

The scream of pain that attacked his heart caused him to hide his face with both hands. What could he have done? He'd had no choice; there was no choice, no decision to be made. His beautiful wife with the golden hair and eyes of green had to die.

Conran sobbed quietly to himself, for the only woman he had ever loved was gone forever. He viewed in his mind, as if it was yesterday, his wife as the wind carried her weightless body 2,500 feet down and into the raging Atlantic below.

Stop! Stop! He must stop now. No more, get in control. Forget. Stop reliving the moment, the moment he had allowed her small delicate hand to slip through his grasp. The moment he had permitted his wife to die. How he still suffered from that time! Conran Blake considered himself hard done by indeed.

God, the pain! It was so much worse now. So much fucking pressure. He thought his head would surely explode. Calm! Calm, must be calm. Hum the lullaby, the familiar rhythmical sounds that had been with him since childhood, the song his mother had always sung to him when he had the pain, the dark moments. The lullaby never failed to ease his tense and aching brain.

CHAPTER 16

Andrew Simpson turned off the computer he was working on and drained the cold dregs that remained in the plastic cup. God, it had been a bitch of a day. A complete waste of time and effort. Tip-off? Some fucking tip off! Barnsey had screwed up big time and Simpson was not happy.

Barnsey was not a bad bloke, and his lack of attention on this case was not really his fault. But it wasn't the first time. Andrew had tried to cover for him and had done so success-fully on many an occasion, but this time he was not sure that he could. After the death of his wife Anna, Alan Barnes had not been himself. Sure, he'd done the year's counselling, taken the recommended time off, yet he still felt dead inside.

Barnsey was, to most people, unremarkable, homely. Yet to his wife he had been a man amongst men: warm, kind, caring. Those had been her prime requirements in a man; the fact that he was short, fat and balding had not mattered.

And then Anna had died in a road traffic accident. It was simply a case of being in the wrong place at the wrong time. Afterwards, Barnsey was, you could say, lost to himself and lost to the Force.

Much as he liked Barnsey, Andrew found it frustrating work-ing alongside someone who had become so blatantly incompe-tent, and was sure it would affect his own plans for promotion. If Barnsey didn't buck his ideas up, he, Andrew, would be stuck in Liverpool forever. The thought was unbearable. Liverpool was too close to the home he had hated and the memories of a brother he sorely missed.

Johnny Simpson hadn't stopped to think about what or who he was getting involved with. What was the big deal? This

Blake guy paid well. Johnny figured he'd do the odd job, a bit of running here and there, bit of smuggling, and he'd have a few bob to spend on the ladies. No problem. What Johnny had failed to realise was that it was not so simple. When you started on the Blake payroll, you stayed on the Blake payroll until further notice. It was for Conran Blake to say if and when you could hang up your boots. You certainly did not just fail to turn up for a job as Johnny had done.

The fresh-faced youth had started to get bored and irritated with the constant demands this outfit was making on his time. Running around airports and stations was not his idea of a good time. Sure, the money allowed him to live a little better but it was only money. Freedom meant more to Johnny. Anyway, times were changing; things were getting harder, more risky. On the last few runs, he had not felt the confidence he once had. Maybe it was the gear itself, the paranoia. He had been hitting it a little hard lately. Next time he would take the gear after the run and not before. This should help him get things into perspective. This Blake guy provided good uncut gear to all his staff - at discounted prices, of course. You just couldn't get the same elsewhere. So what if people said things? Just rumours, people loved rumours.

It was said that this guy Blake had once been married. They said he'd loved his wife, almost to distraction. Loved her so much he'd killed her. Now did that make sense? thought Johnny. Kill because you love so much? No, these were just stories, ghost stories. They say she had taken a lover, they had planned to run away together, Ireland, if he remembered the tales correctly. Something had happened and Blake had taken the head of her lover then chucked her off some cliff. Crazy, ha?

On this particular day Johnny Simpson had been given strict instructions to meet Gregory Scott, Blake's henchman, in The Reading Rooms, a privately owned Gentlemen's Club Blake had frequented for some years and from where he ran most of this outfit. But on this day Johnny had felt, well, sort of lazy. It had been an effort to get out of bed and that was not just because Tanya felt so soft and smooth, her young skin brushing against his. It had nothing to do with that. You never let a woman get in the way of business, did you? At least that's what the boys said, but Johnny thought different. What was so wrong with liking a woman? He liked to be in the company of females. Today he would stay in bed and enjoy the feel of her and her tender body sliding all over him once again. Blake and Scott could go hang; he was not in the mood to play Mafiosi today.

Johnny had escaped the wrath of Conran Blake on two previous occasions for 'insubordination' - otherwise known as failing in his duties. It was not a failure to be repeated. To be unreliable was like being a grass in the eyes of Conran Blake and Gregory Scott. Young Johnny Simpson had simply been asked to drive. What was so difficult about that?

So where the fuck was he? thought Gregory Scott, who had been looking forward to this job. It had been some time since he'd administered a little discipline and he was quite looking forward to the occasion. An example had to be set. Things were getting very sloppy. A quick dash down the A1, a pint and a light lunch, onto the perpetrator's house to administer a reminder of who was who by way of the old and much-loved machete routine, then home in time for tea. A man of his standing could not be expected to drive himself and perform to the standard required. It was simply unheard of. After all, Scott looked upon himself as an artist of sorts. Johnny had let the company down. Scott was disappointed. A visit was in order.

Tanya snuggled closer and closer into the hot, moist body of the boy she loved. Yes, loved. This was the only man she had ever given herself to heart, body and soul. It was Johnny Simpson for her, or no-one. So her friends had lots of lovers. Tanya Morris was not like the other girls in the concrete jungle. No she was, well, quiet. Looking into his face, his eyes shut and his body still close to hers, she longed to open her heart to him. Yet what if he ran scared? After all, this guy was a known womaniser. Free of spirit was good old Johnny boy; everyone loved him and she was under no illusions that she was the only woman he dated or slept with. But hey! Everyone had to settle down at some point, didn't they? Even guys like Johnny. She'd be good to him, take care of him, love him, bear him children, be a good and loyal wife to him.

Oh God! It was now or never and if Johnny said no, then... Better not to think like that. At this moment of tranquillity, Tanya felt a love that gripped her whole being. The strength of it sent a tear trickling down her smooth young cheeks. Love could make you cry. Love was like that.

It was during this tender moment that the door banged violently open, startling the life out of the two naked lovers entwined together. Like a rag doll, Scott took the screaming girl by the hair and flung her to her knees. As she landed on all fours, her head bent forward, Scott administered a bullet into the neck of Tanya Morris. Johnny managed a final death-cry as Gregory Scott caused his genitalia to pebble-dash the room. It had taken just the one bullet each. Fuck, that was a rush, thought Scott, who decided he quite fancied a pizza.

CHAPTER 17

The salad sat untouched in the crystal bowl, its leaves starting to wilt at the edges, crowned with tomatoes that no longer seemed as succulent and refreshing as they had four hours ago when they were prepared. What could be said of the once-fresh bread? she thought as she bounced it off the table. Mary Jayne felt like the drooping salad. It had taken some effort to put on the stockings and black sleek dress. It had taken love to transform herself into a vision of sexy sophistication after a hard day spent running around the park after the children; a day spent cleaning and taking care of her kids. Still, she liked to please her man. She was aware that Andrew liked her to look her best at all times. Andrew did not like sloppiness. Mary Jayne understood this, as she understood his need for order and stability in his life at the end of a day.

Remembering her husband's apparent tension as he had driven off that morning, Mary Jayne was determined to put a smile on those dark, alluring features.

It was now 10.30pm and, like the meal she had prepared, she would have to wait. At 10'45 the front door slammed shut and an exhausted Andrew Simpson threw his coat on the hook. He knew where she would be and headed straight for the kitchen.

'Darling, I'm sorry it's so late. Hell, it's been a bitch of a day. Barnsey really is going to have to get it together. I'm sorry'

'Never mind,' she murmured, hiding her disappointment. Such was her responsibility as the wife of a policeman. Blowing out the candles that now burnt at half-mast, she went upstairs to run him a soothing bath. Andrew Simpson sat down on the large leather Chesterfield and fell into a deep sleep.

Removing her stockings and black lace panties, Mary Jayne allowed her fingers to trace the curves of her body, finally resting between her thighs and slowly touching her clitoris. Hmm, the tender touch of her own gentle fingers helped ease the tension. Lying back on the large bed adorned with its brilliant white duvet cover and swaddling pillows, she breathed a soft sigh of pleasure. Fantasies she did not dare speak of danced around in her mind. Feeling safe to explore at her leisure, eyelids closed tightly to keep her fantasies locked inside her imagination, to dance alone and free, the warm slippery liquid allowed her fingers to enter gently, rhythmically stroking to the pace of her dreams. The fantasies grew more vivid as the muscles of her internal organs began to grow taut and she reached perfect orgasm. Now the dance ended and Mary Jayne began to drift off, her husband snoring gently at her side, her fantasies safely put away till next time.

The next day was Sunday. A day for coffee and breakfast in bed, a day to litter the duvet with the morning newspapers. Thank God, she thought. Tomorrow, hopefully, Barnsey would not phone. Tomorrow, hopefully, the dammed pager would not go off and Mary Jayne would have her husband at home for the whole day. The children would not be allowed out of their rooms till 9am. On Sunday mornings, Andrew Simpson liked his children to read something that would inform and educate their young minds. Mrs Simpson understood the benefits of this. The children did not.

Conran Blake coughed and puked, missing the basin altogether and creating a mess on the carpet. No matter, Bella his housemaid would clear it up. Oh yes, she would. Bella, whose youth and beauty had lasted but moments, or so it seemed. A long time ago, when her lips had been dull and moist, her skin dove-white; she had run from Conran Blake.

It was her timing that had been off. Had Bella chosen a better moment, instead of the day Conran had gone to Ireland to chase his goody-goody wife, she would have got clean away. Nothing could have warned Bella that he would go so far to bring her back. The fact that he had paid so much attention to her absence upon his return from Ireland had confused her. Bella knew Blake did not, would not and could not love her. Fact. It was simply that nobody ran away from Conran Blake, nobody left without his permission. Two women had tried to reject him. The first was dead, taking with her any human pity Blake had ever felt.

The second, Bella, was not so fortunate. Scott had brought her back from a nearby brothel, along with a grand in cash she had lifted from Blake. Silly Bella had regretted her actions. Well, in truth she was forced to regret her actions, and to this day her hair had never grown as it once had, thick and healthy.

Still, free coke made anything worthwhile. To be without and go cold turkey was unthinkable. Death would be preferable. After all, why go through the fever, the sickness, the pounding headaches, the confusion? Oh yes to be without the powder was not an option now. Besides, why be clean and together? Who cared enough? No-one: cruel but true. The coke helped her get by get through the days. How else would she cope with the abuse, the venom that spurted out of his mouth? She was a whore, a slut, a nothing. Abuse was her life. But it was when he spoke of her, his wife, that it really angered her. When he compared her to Morgan, Morgan, beautiful and saintly Morgan, the dead Morgan. To die young, beautiful and free would have been her choice, if only she'd had the luxury of one. Blake kept Bella nearby purely to punish her for his shit of a life.

Standing over the tanned, masculine torso, Bella could not deny he had a youthful physique. Only his greying hair betrayed his descent into middle age.

'Clean this place up, bitch!'

'Fuck you!' she snarled back, dodging the expected blow. If they could see him now, right now, his pants around his ankles and puke still lingering around his lips. Not a nice sight to behold. The great Conran Blake? Yea, like everyone, God farted.

Too many drinks, that was the problem. It couldn't possibly be the coke he had snorted last night. So far the weekend had been hectic. A new consignment had come in and the usual shit with it. His men had been behaving like paranoid school children. Had he not told them to trust him? Hadn't he told them that everything was under control? Total lack of faith, that's what it was, total lack of faith. Maybe Scott needed his arse kicking. Tell him to instil a little more discipline; after all, Conran had other things to do. Being disturbed in the middle of the night was annoying, especially when he had his head in the best bit of fanny he'd touched in some time. This girl had a cunt like the Venus de Milo and a taste to match.

Barnsey! All this was over Barnsey. Fuck, he'd been serving Barnsey with cash up front and the odd line of coke for years. Couldn't they figure it out? The campaign had been Barnsey's idea. Tell the idiots at CID he'd had a tip-off, then go in the other direction. Coke enters country, no probs. Barnsey. Why were they all scared of Barnsey? Blake owned Barnsey down to the dick. Yea, he'd even given him the bitch Bella to keep him happy. And it paid. You could never have too many police on the pay-roll; it made good business sense.

Bella hated the little fat copper. She reckoned he was fucked in the head. He had made her look a fool, a right bloody idiot, to be exact. That night she'd smelled the liquor on his hot and rancid breath. The stench of his dripping sweat was nauseating. He had tied her to the bed face down, then started to cry and cry like a baby, sobbing for all his worth, whimpering to himself like a baby.

'Dead! Oh God! Dead! No more, I'll never see you again, Anna. Anna! I hate life, hate this bitch, this dirty bitch. No, not the cunt. Never the cunt. Only with you, Anna, my love, only with you.'

Barnsey went on to run his tragically small penis right into Bella's jacksey. When it was all over, still sobbing, still crying, he had taken a blade and casually shaved off both of her eyebrows. Even though it had been some time since Bella had looked remotely attractive, she looked a right cunt now. The once toned thighs were now saggy, the small breasts had seen

better days. Her hair was short simply because it grew out-
wards and in patches. The external cold sores always made her
lips look thin and scrawny. Perhaps once she had been considered cute in an elfish sort of way, but now the eyes were barren,
sunken and lifeless. It wasn't much better on the inside. The
tongue was badly ulcerated, caused by the coke or amphetamines she often took orally now.

Barnsey was losing it. There had been a dinner party last
night at the big house in Birkenhead, a house Blake had bought
on the opening of his new casino. The house was not unlike the
old one in Orrell, in fact, similar in many ways. A big old dwelling with a classic Victorian look. It had previously belonged to
a mad old American woman, who had loved and adored everything English, including the Royal family. So the house did
have that air of Victorian wealth about it. For Blake it was ideal
town house, perfect, not too far from the casino and the city
centre, yet far enough to be out of the hustle and bustle of the
main streets.

His previous house had been home to his mother and her
mother before that, so he had been proud to make it his marital
home. Alas, once the tragedy had happened he could no longer
bear the sight of it. Whereas once it had felt safe and peaceful,
now all he could remember were bad times. His memories of
a contented childhood, those secluded days of safety held close
to his mother's breast, were now just fleeting. The joys of married life, too, were no more than glancing moments. It had all
started to go wrong the day their son had died a cot death.

Bella had been told to act as waitress to the few well-chosen
VIP guests. Ambassadors and heads of large corporations were
all like family to the Blake Empire, and acted as protection for
him. Conran Blake held court with such style.

The grand dining room had looked magnificent with its silver candlesticks and silver cutlery. A table set for a prince. A
first-class chef had been brought in for the occasion, along with
the finest wines and champagnes. Whores had been hand-picked
by Blake, notable for their contrasting looks: dark-skinned, light-

skinned, blondes, brunettes. They were like a set of chess pieces. For himself he had chosen a dark girl with large brown eyes, called... Well, it didn't matter, she was gone now; he had taken his pleasure and wanted some sleep. Damn the drink! He hated drinking. Too much champagne always gave him a terrible hangover that would last all day.

Barnsey sat rigid at Conran Blake's breakfast table, along with the other VIPs who had stayed the night. Why had he drunk so much? It was all very well attending dinner but staying overnight, the involvement was too much and scared him. What if someone saw him leaving? This was Liverpool after all, his own patch, not Manchester, his normal meeting place with Blake. He was losing it. This was madness. Go. He wanted to get away and quick; he was also knackered and his dick hurt. Kaco had been a frisky little Japanese girl with a nifty pelvic thrust to die for. She had worn him out big time.

Bella, having cleaned up the puke, began to serve breakfast without bothering to wash her hands first. Dishing out bacon and eggs from a large silver tureen, she allowed just a little hot butter to drop on to Barnsey's balding head. Yea, take that, she thought as the bastard winced in pain. Don't remember me, do ya, shit head? she thought.

Blake entered just in time to stop Bella pouring hot coffee all over the fat little git's head.

'Gentlemen, I trust you slept well?' Positive grunts came from all angles, an enthusiastic response to their host's good taste and breeding.

Breakfast done with, people started to bid farewell. Barnsey spied his chance to be out of it. But Conran had spotted him and called him over.

'Mr Barnes, if you could possible give me a couple of moments, perhaps Bella has prepared coffee for us in the library'.

Oh Jesus! Fuck, his nerves would not stand it, he was in too deep. Way too deep. He needed a line just to get him through it.

Trembling, they entered the enormous library decorated with books, a truly magnificent display. Blake was a highly educated, well-read man and someone who was similarly inclined would no doubt have found the place a sheer delight. But Barnsey was no bookworm, and this was no time for literature.

'Now,' smiled Conran, 'my men tell me that last night, they saw what could have been one or two of your chaps in uniform, and it seemed as if they were lying in wait. I believe you gave the all clear, Mr Barnes?'

'It's just a coincidence, Mr Conran. I would have stopped the show if I thought for a minute a pull was likely.'

Blake sat behind his big oak desk and talked as he nonchalantly playing with a cigarette lighter made in the shape of deck of cards, a present from the Colombian Ambassador. Bella listened outside, her ear plastered to the door, and hoped that Barnsey would get it in the head just like the last guy to cross Blake. It would serve him right.

At that moment, Gregory Scott tore her away by her hair and strode into the library. He was a powerfully-built, vicious-looking man. One would never have guessed by looking at him that his particular fetish was young, sweet-looking boys.

The sight of Scott told Barnsey that Blake was seriously pissed off.

'Mr Barnes, I must be frank with you. Near misses are not good enough. The sight of your chaps makes my chaps nervous and then they start to bother me and I simply do not have the time to fuck around.' Conran could feel the pain start to grow in his head. It was a warning to stay calm and not get worked up. 'Why do I pay you?'

'I can assure you, Mr Blake, it was a coincidence, really. They were simply beat police who know nothing, I can assure you.'

'On the contrary, Mr Barnes, it's my chap here you need to assure. Gregory can be very... shall we say *demonstrative*, particularly when nervous. Now this time I will talk my good friend here into allowing you the benefit of the doubt. But be sure you will be watched closely. Good day to you, Mr Barnes.'

Barnsey left just as the piss started to display a damp patch on his trousers.

CHAPTER 18

Monday morning brought all the usual chaos. Kids off to school armed with lunch boxes and happy smiles on their cherubic faces. Dad had left some hours earlier. The kids liked it that way; it meant they could giggle at the breakfast table and eat chocolate-coated cereal instead of the oats Dad insisted were good for them.

The school bus pulled away just as the post dropped onto the thick pile carpet. Brown window envelopes caused Mary Jayne no concern as she filed them away into the big writing desk in her husband's study, a serious and sombre place, suitable for its purpose. A large teak desk, walls of books and a rather dominant high-backed chair were its main features. A lamp loomed over the middle of the desk, throwing a small pool of light. All in all it was a dull and depressing room.

What a house they lived in, large beautifully furnished. Any show house would have seemed dull in comparison. Surely any woman would have killed for the large carved oak kitchen, the long living room and its great full-length windows dressed in finest fabric. The pure wool, white carpet spoke of softness and luxury to the feet on a cold winter's evening. The living flame fire that stood in the centre of the room, surrounded by a large marble hearth, was deliciously inviting. Indeed, it was a fine house.

Mary Jayne traced her fingers along the oak preparation services. Nice, she thought, but not really to her taste. Something simpler would have suited her. But not Andrew.

All was still and quiet but for the boiling of the kettle on the large Aga stove (that, too, had been Andrew's idea). She did not really want a coffee; it simply killed a moment in her day, gave her one moment less to think about her lost career as a solicitor. Nine-to-five office hours, a quick lunch consisting of a sandwich whilst preparing for court. She remembered the hustle and bustle of rush hour, the hilarity of office banter, that taste of success, the bitter taste of inevitable failures. Above all, she remembered the buzz of being a part of something, being involved, belonging.

Had she not met Andrew, she wondered what her life would have been like. Not that she regretted anything. Good God, no! Didn't she have it all? Well, didn't she? Marrying her first love had made sense. After all, nothing could be better. Andrew was charming and successful, handsome and generous. Okay, in an ideal word perhaps it would have been nice to have gained a little more experience of the opposite sex, but still, what could be better than this? Her husband was a real catch. Being pregnant so soon had been a shock to her but not to Andrew, and somehow his enthusiasm had washed off on her. Saying goodbye to her career as a solicitor had been hard. Still, she harboured hopes of returning to work after perhaps a year or so.

Sipping her coffee, Mary Jayne focused her memory on her younger days, days spent on Achill Island. She was once again the ever-energetic child, dressed in jeans and a T-shirt, running wild around the island, in and out of neighbours' houses, bidding good morning, good day. Chasing the donkeys that freely roamed the island, dodging the streams and bog land, fighting with old Mrs Malley's geese and winding them up, causing an outbreak of wild cackling screams.

'Mary Jayne, will you be gone now before I take a broom to you! I swear one day they'll catch you, to be sure they will. It'll be your own doing when they bite ya!'

Farming the land as her Uncle Robert did held no interest for her, nor had she enjoyed bringing in the turf. Clumps of smelly dirty earth were hardly inspiring! Uncle Robert swore she was not an Achill Islander.

'Mary Jayne, your own mother could do the work of a man

when it came to digging turf. Don't be such a pansy and get your back into it, girl.'

How she had sulked and moaned, wishing away the days until she could escape to the sanctity of the Minuan cliffs, the only place she had ever felt any real sense of belonging. With nothing more than a fondness for the past, Mary Jayne had hurriedly left Achill Island, thinking she was saying goodbye to loneliness forever. Yet now it seemed she was lonelier than ever. After all you can be in a room loved by a hundred people and still feel lonely.

Dropping her gloomy thoughts, she sat back to scan the local paper.

Conran Blake would have preferred to sleep late. Last night had been exhausting though therapeutic. Wendy had put everything into perspective for him, just like his mother used to. Alas, duty called once again in the form of golf with the Chief Executive of Liverpool City Council, a rematch; this guy was determined to thrash Conran. There'd be drinks in the bar afterwards, then lunch. Conran often held court at the golf club. To be seen with him meant you really were the pick of the crop. His weaknesses were well hidden under the classy, aristocratic image he liked to portray.

Yet, just as a drinker needs a drink and a junkie a fix, Blake needed to exercise his fetish. For this he would call upon the services of Wendy. A few years younger than he, Wendy had been in his employ since the early days at Billings Casino. When the door closed on the casino patrons and staff, Wendy would often stay behind. The cellars were cold, dark dingy places at the bottom of Eagle Palace, the second in a chain of three casinos based in Liverpool. The darkness suited Blake for he liked no real light, no daylight.

The woman was dressed in matronly attire, her breasts heaving underneath the heavy blouse and pinny, her hair scraped back, legs encased in thick stockings, her arms folded as if she was vexed. The figure in the corner of the room facing the wall shivered as little goose bumps appeared on his bare buttocks. The crisp white shirt, complete with tie, hung just below his waist. The black silk stockings shielded his legs a little.

'Now, if you continue to be a naughty boy, Mummy will have to thrash you and make you wear girls' clothes at school. Pull your stockings up just like a good girl.' The voice was firm and held the note of a threat. Approaching the figure facing the wall, Wendy brought her hand slap down onto the bottom of the naughty boy, who winced with pain.

'You're a very bad boy!' *Slap*, again and again. 'I can see I'm going to have to be stern with you.' Now sitting, the woman commanded the boy to lie across her. Talking a pair of lace panties out of her pinny pocket, she slipped them over his legs and buttocks.

'Now, naughty boy, I have prepared you to be punished.' Pulling down the knickers just to the base of his bottom, Wendy felt between his legs, reaching the penis that thrust out long and hard.

'This will never do!' With a long, thin cane, Wendy whipped his bottom until it was very red and sore. The figure started to whimper.

'I'm sorry, Mummy, I'm sorry. I'll be good, honest I will. Please don't punish me any more.'

Moving the figure on to the floor and kneeling down opposite, with one chubby hand she pressed the searching mouth of the boy hard against her nipple that was just visible against her blouse. Taking his penis, she began to rub up and down, up and down. His dick ached to shoot its bursting liquid that began to rise from deep within his loins. He sucked the nipple harder, almost biting. God, it was coming as the hand that wanked it grew faster, faster, more furious in its pulling. Spunk shot through the end of his cock, drenching the stockings.

It was over. Wendy tucked away her breast, turned and left. Not a word was spoken or passed between the two. Wendy was loyal. Blake tore off the stockings and the panties that had now made their way between his knees. He could no longer bear the sight of them.

As always Conran won hands down on the golf course, much to the dismay of William Liptrot, Leader of the Council. This would mean the champagne was on him again. Still, he could put it down to his expense account.

'A splendid game, William, that was quite some fight you put up'.

'You flatter me, Conran, really, there's no need'

'Oh, William, not at all. I'm just on a roll, it seems'.

'Do let's go and have some champagne.'

'After you,' grinned Conran, in public ever the epitome of fine manners and breeding.

Putting down the newspaper, Mary Jayne read with excitement that tickets to the opera were still available. What a treat that would be! Talking Andrew into taking her would certainly be worth a try - after all, this was opening night, a real event for the D'Oley Carte Opera company, an opportunity not to be missed. It was only ever in emergencies that she phoned her husband at the office, and she considered this was one. As she had hoped, she managed to overcome his initial reluctance with her girlish excitement.

'Oh Andrew, please they're performing Carmen! I couldn't bear to let the chance pass us by. Please say yes, darling! Barnsey could sit for the kids.'

'Children, Mary Jayne, children'.

'Children. Oh, just this once, darling!'

'Okay, okay we'll go. Just calm down!'

'Ha!' she screamed aloud and into the phone. 'Andrew Simpson, I love you.'

Dribbling salad cream over the last of the smoked salmon, William Liptrot gorged himself. Blake looked upon the scene with utter disgust and an urge to retch. My God, Liptrot was a philistine when all was said and done. Give the bastard a bag of chips and he'd be more at home than in the golf club.

'Oh, by the way,' Liptrot rasped, his mouth full. 'I have two tickets for the D'Oley Carte Opera this evening, they're performing Carmen. Can you use them? Blessed wife's cried off with the usual haemorrhoids - can't sit for long!'

That created a nice picture in Blake's head, imagining what the wife of the small pot-bellied, double-chinned man would look like. A pot-bellied, double-chinned, female version of him, no doubt, with thighs that chaffed together, creating sweat and ulcers. Huge flabby buttocks, creating a nice mound for the piles to flourish in. That image was enough - time to get the fuck out of there and take those blasted tickets with him if he had to.

God! What a day. What a fucking awful, ugly day. Full of ugly people: Bella with her pox-ridden face, then fat little Liptrot. Was there to be no more beauty in his life, no real beauty, pure beauty just like Morgan had possessed? Morgan, his wife, his wife. The pain hit his temples and went to take his vision. He craved beauty: not necessarily the perfect face and body (though that, he admitted, never hurt), but true inner beauty. Never again would he love and be loved as a man like himself deserved to be. Morgan had loved him at first, truly loved him, he was certain of that. There had been moments of such sweetness, such pleasure, such innocence.

In his life he had experienced only two real loves, both brief. His mother, though strict and perhaps at times a little old-fashioned, had loved him dearly, even desperately. Mother had protected him from himself as best she could. Protected him from the sins he now committed at his leisure. The beatings, the times she had locked him in cupboards and other small places: it had all been because she loved him. Life had been cruel to Miss Blake. As a child of fourteen, her body had been ravaged at the lustful hands of a local boy. Conran was the bruised fruit of her sin. Her son must be taught to deny the urges and stay pure, control his carnal desire, and the only way to do this was to keep him away from humanity and all its filth and temptation.

And so Miss Blake had died. Her son was a somewhat strange boy, though bright and advanced for his thirteen years.

His inheritance had allowed the best psychiatric care to help him readjust and come to terms with his mother's death. After much counselling, Conran Blake, once hidden to the outside world, was on his way to becoming a well adjusted young man with a future.

University was a happy time for him until the executors of his mother's will put a stop to his frivolous spending. Blake took the odd bit of coke with his pals, snorted the odd line here and there and enjoyed himself. But, he was told, this would all have to stop. Of course it did not. The lack of funds simply motivated the young Blake to build an empire he alone would control; where he alone would call the shots.

Conran Blake had everything - almost. But he craved beauty, a quality he had experienced for only fleeting moments. All around him people demanded, lied and cheated. Friendships were bought and sold. Beauty was nowhere to be found in his life. Perhaps a trip to the opera would provide a little.

Even the thought of sitting through more than two hours of opera was a nightmare for Andrew Simpson. Pleasure for him would have been a cosy night in. If Mary Jayne craved music, he would be more than happy to play a selection of his Barry White LPs. He could always say Barnsey wasn't available to baby-sit but that would be dishonest. Walking into the house, he suddenly had an idea.

'Andrew, the bath's ready for you darling. I'm up here.'

'What? Oh yea.'

Mary Jayne sensed the lack of enthusiasm in his voice; it put her on edge. Hell, he might call the evening off. Eyes up to heaven, she begged the good lord not to let him do that. Was she being selfish? Well maybe, just this once.

'Mary Jayne,' he called up the stairs. 'Look, I'm sorry...'

She was standing at the top of the stairs, and he read her instant disappointment.

'Look, Barnsey will take you, he never gets out and it would do him good. Darling, I'm just too tired and you know how I fidget in my seat at these things.'

The deal was done. Well, it was okay as long as she got to wallow in the beauty of the opera. Barnsey agreed. Maybe he was going soft but Mrs Simpson wasn't that bad. What the hell, best bib and tucker, a snort of powder in the Simpsons' bathroom and he would be in the mood.

Conran could have taken any one of his many mistresses to the event. The question that arose in his mind was: why? True, they where good for a fuck, a dance, that type of thing, but the opera? No. On this occasion he would go alone, escorted by his own thoughts. Perhaps a song from Carmen would help cheer his melancholy mood.

'Well, do I look okay'?

Her hair tumbled in silky, bouncy curls on to the slender shoulders and beyond. From the bottom of the stairs he could see how her lips shone red with moisture. Excitement shone from the black eyes. Off-the-shoulder, curving round her breasts, the black lace dress seemed to caress her body all the way down to her waist, picked up slightly on the hips and came to a halt just below the knees. He was a lucky man. Was he mad not to be escorting this creature into the night? Still, Barnsey would take care of her, his jewel.

Barnsey looked like a little fat penguin, but Mary Jayne thought he looked cute. The opera was all it had promised to be. Bizet's Carmen was vibrant and wild, the music inspiring and the voice of the female lead brimmed with unspoken passion. The character of Carmen was exciting as she was portrayed as a frivolous girl, wild with her own beauty and dangerously attractive. The girl playing the lead was flirtatious, taunting, excellent in her role as a wanton lover of men. Her lover Don Jose was tall, strong and powerful, a corporal of the Dragoon Guards brought to his knees by the power of a woman and his own need for her.

Secretly, Mary Jayne wondered how it might feel to be wanted with such abandoned passion, to be a femme fatale. As an adult she had never really been frivolous and flirtatious; even the thought of it made her blush. Mothers did not think like that; there was no nook for such a fantasy character as Carmen in her role as mother.

The final scene pitted lover against lover, passion fighting passion to result in death - the death of Don Jose, killed by his own anger, hatred and jealousy. After spilling the blood of Carmen, her lover sought his own death at the hands of an angry mob, for without love he was nothing and cared nothing for life. A bloody, bloody state of affairs.

The applause was rapturous as the audience stood roaring its approval.

He had first noticed her during Act Two. His eyes had been drawn to this young woman sitting three seats away from him, who was clearly drowning in the drama unfolding on-stage. She was entranced by the music, the dancing, like a child in a pantomime or a fairytale. From her profile, he could see that emotion was running through her heart like a raging fire, as she perched on the edge of her seat, her body straining forward in enthusiasm. It made him long to calm her. It was this capacity to feel that had aroused his interest. He wondered who was with this strange child-like woman, for his view of the entire row was not good.

People began to leave. She took her shawl and stood, ready to exit. As she made her way up the aisle, her shawl fell to the floor.

A tall, distinguished-looking man kindly retrieved it for her. 'Let me get that for you.'

His voice was warm and cultured. Barnsey realised at once who it was, and dodged behind a man following him, pretending he had left something behind on the seat. Jesus! he thought, not Blake, not here. Fuck! Must get out and quick. Must get away without being seen. Barnsey made a quick exit via the opposite aisle. Mary Jayne did not notice at first that her escort had disappeared.

Placing the shawl in her hands, his touch lingered upon her. She blushed.

'Did you enjoy the opera? I must say you looked enthralled,' said Conran Blake.

'Oh! It was wonderful, really I could see it all over again. Don't you think it was simply magical?'

'Yes indeed. Did your husband enjoy it too?'

'No, no this isn't my husband.' She turned around to introduce Barnsey but he was gone. 'Oh! My escort seems to have vanished. My husband doesn't share my love for opera so we more or less had to bribe a family friend to escort me.'

He looked into her eyes, and saw such darkness and mystery there. He was transfixed for a moment. She felt the burn of his gaze. It caused her to gasp for breath. Someone had just walked over her grave.

'Well, I'd better find my escort, he must be front of house somewhere. It appears I'm holding the queue up. Thank you for my shawl.'

'Think nothing of it.'

The October air was stiff with threats of cold winter weather to come. Barnsey had flagged a taxi down and, on seeing Mary Jayne emerge from the crowd alone, he hastily opened the door and hustled her on to the back seat. What the hell was Blake doing there? All of a sudden the cunt was an opera buff!

The ride back to Port Sunlight took twenty minutes, yet it seemed like only moments to Mary Jayne, whose thoughts kept lingering on the man she had just met. There was something about him, a feeling she had, and his memory and voice would not leave her. She did not say a word during the trip - she just kept smiling to herself all the way home.

CHAPTER 19

Mid-December brought all the gaiety of Christmas. Jingle bells and the smell of roasted chestnuts filled the cold winter air. Santa Claus ho-ho-hoed and the bells of Christmas rang out, promising joy and prosperity to all. St James's Church boasted a congregation any man of God would be proud of. Spilling out onto the porch, families merrily huddled close together to sing an array of Christmas carols. This was a special thanksgiving service, celebrating the good work of local charities and the kind men and women who gave their time freely. It was also a time to thank local business people for there kind donations. Yes, a time to thank one and all.

Conran Blake was no exception to this and felt himself a pillar of the community as he took his place in the front pew of St James's RC Church. He relished the opportunity to deliver his allocated reading to the congregation of 'nice people'.

Mary Jayne had cringed when Father Davies had asked her to read in the coming Celebratory Christmas Mass. Snipping the odd stem off the church flowers was one thing, but a reading? But, as was the tradition, one did not argue with a priest. Mary Jayne sat four pews down from the front. Blake sat up front near to the alter along with council leaders and other community members.

The church choir, accompanied by the local school children, did justice to 'Away In A Manger'. Conran thanked them on behalf of Father Davies and addressed the congregation with an easy style and perfect delivery. And had all the angels of hell been present that evening, they could have not helped but fall for the sincerity of Mr Blake. Here was a man who truly felt for the less fortunate. His voice dripped with compassion.

'Now, good people I believe we have a reading from the Ladies, Church Group, thank you.' He took his seat.

Mary Jayne approached the alter, realising that she had paid no attention at all to anything that had gone before, due to nerves. Silly, she thought, but anyway, now it was her turn. Catherine and David sat beside their father, who looked at his wife with pride. She looked regal, divine and alluring all at the same time.

Mary Jayne read the bidding prayers. 'We give thanks to the Lord for the goodness of the people. 'Lord hear us'

The congregation echoed: 'Lord, graciously hear us.'

Conran Blake stared. It was the woman from the theatre. The sincerity of her compelling tones sifted through his head. It was as if his heart had stopped. When her reading was over, she stepped elegantly down from the pulpit and took her seat. Father Davies thanked the congregation for their attendance, he thanked the readers and the sponsors and, of course, the choir.

Conran had not known that the flowers he was to present were for Mary Jayne. He had expected to be handing them to some old washerwoman. He became suddenly shy. Receiving the flowers, she too recognised him from the night at the opera. She was struck again by how handsome he was, how strong the look in his eyes was, even if it was slightly strange.

The lights on the alter flickered as if touched by a light gentle breeze. Burning red, the candles perfumed the air with wax. Her nipples stood erect, waiting for his touch, his attention. Shadows danced across her nakedness. He folded her in his arms and laid her upon the Altar of Christ. Not yet would he greet the opening that lay in wait for him; not yet would she feel his desire penetrate her. Looking down upon her, he worshipped the sculptured body. He traced his fingers across her lips; she moaned, longing to be his pleasure. His fingers lightly touched her skin as he traced her form down to the inner thighs. She shuddered and moaned, her thoughts now of loving, her body almost in spasms with anticipation. Tasting her, licking her, she became his elixir to life and his lust grew and demanded more. For such was his need of her. And the eyes of God looked down upon them.

His cock was stiff and fit to burst. It was always like this when he woke up with a hard-on. Again his head, the sharp stabbing pains grabbed at his temples. He hummed the lullaby that would ease his thoughts as always.

'Hush little baby, don't say a word, poppa's gonna buy you a mocking bird, and if that mocking bird don't sing, poppa's gonna buy you a diamond ring.'

Damn the dream! he thought as he struggled to return to that place of ecstasy. For sleep would not come back to him.

Mary Jayne hated herself, for her thoughts were no longer her own and she had no control over them. His eyes would not leave her. They mocked her somehow. The very nature of her thoughts was immoral and deceiving.

Andrew Simpson had thought the church event perfect. He had achieved and indeed was living his dream; living the life he had made sure was a million miles away from the squalor and poverty he had known as a child. Last night had said it all for him: his children sitting well dressed at the side of him, his perfect wife playing a part in the holy event at Yuletide. Ah yes, he thought, all was as he would have it. The perfect wholesome family and it belonged to him, Andrew Simpson. Members of the local community looked on the sight approvingly and with a fondness for this good Catholic family. Praised was heaped upon his children. Weren't they growing up! How the boy looked like his father! And the girl, as pretty as her mother! Andrew Simpson relished it all.

It had started that night. As Andrew held his arms out to be loved, she had come to him and given herself to the man she had married and sworn to love forever. He pulled her close. No doubt she was sure of his love, yet sometimes, just sometimes, she felt in his touch a coldness that scared her. Tonight he was not gentle. Tonight he was strong and urgent in his lovemaking. That was okay; she was flattered. Twisting and turning, she tried to be rid of the eyes of the stranger, yet she could not. They burned her and looked deep into her soul. She was thinking about another man as her husband loved her. Try as she might, on this night she was not thinking about Andrew Simpson.

Christmas was a tastefully exquisite affair in the Simpson household, from formal dinner parties to cocktail evenings. Andrew insisted on playing host to the powers-that-be, from local politicians to high-ranking members of his beloved constabulary. Andrew would describe these events as cultured and civilised, befitting his status.

The sound of carols classically sung filtered through the long hall way and as far as the front door, audible to the two children who stood like little soldiers dressed in finery to greet their guests.

'Darling, you really do need to come downstairs now. It's almost 7.30. For goodness sake, what on earth are you doing?' called Andrew, now getting quite impatient with his wife. He liked things to be organised, and it was imperative his wife and children were standing with him, ready to welcome his guests.

'David, if you fiddle with that tie one more time you and I are going to have one of little private meetings. Do I make myself clear?'

David, knowing only too well that his father was not to be trifled with, shuddered and responded with a 'Sorry, Father'.

'Mary Jayne, downstairs! Now!'

She didn't want to come downstairs. She was dreading another night of polite chitchat, another night of running backwards and forwards to the kitchen preparing canapés and such like. Mary Jayne was tired and longed to have a quiet Christmas with her family instead of the eternal round of guests and dinner parties her husband insisted on.

Now, flustered and panic-stricken, the mother appeared at in the hallway desperately trying to apply her lipstick without the use of a mirror.

'It's just not good enough, Mary Jayne. Really, you have all day to get organised, you simply must try harder.'

Sometimes she could get really angry with her husband.

Guest arrived and marvelled at the values of a good Christian family. What fine children and how well mannered; what a splendid example of a fine English family! It was good to see some of the old traditional family values.

'Andrew, what a credit to you!' cried William Liptrot Leader of the Council.

'Oh! One does ones best,' Andrew responded.

Mary Jayne wondered why she bothered. It seemed her husband could do the job of mother and father alone. Perhaps she wasn't needed at all.

Bathing in praise, Andrew was in a good mood as the rest of the evening went without a hitch, though he must remember to mention the canapés to Mary Jayne. Not quite as good as last year's. Room for improvement.

Playing the part as well as she could, Mary Jayne smiled, laughed and charmed the people her husband held so dear, right up to the departure of the last guest. No sooner had the door closed than she breathed a sigh of relief. Andrew kissed and congratulated her on the evening's success, though he was indeed quite pleased with himself. They could all now relax: the master was happy. That's all that mattered.

The plane touched down. Liverpool Airport was quiet, no crowds or rowdy holidaymakers to deal with. Literally off the plane and into the awaiting car. Conran had insisted upon Spain, it eased the pain. Christmas was never as in-your-face in a foreign country. The winter sun seemed to stop the memories of Christmas spent in Scotland with Morgan. Yes, Spain dulled the memory.

Gregory Scott, driving his master home, gave a complete update on his affairs. Nothing much to report. True, they'd had to give one of their own a good caning before escorting him out of the country and out of harm's way. Still, his wife and children could write to him. Of course the second option available to Tony had been no option at all. It was sad when long-term employees let you down. Was loyalty such an old fashioned value? Honestly, you pay well, you take care of your own, and this is how they repay you. They take a little here and a little there, and before you know it these little cash incentives became big money. Conran Blake's money. It was never a good idea. He always found out.

CHAPTER 20

Conran thought he looked refreshed, not tanned but refreshed. The eyes seemed brighter than they had been and the extra pound or two he carried easily. Espana had served him well as a retreat from all the Christmas festivities. Being abroad had seen him through his saddest and loneliest time.

But now, once again his sleep was tortured. Just as a thousand times before, his dream had taken him to the Minaun cliffs, and again he was forced to allow the small hand to slip from his grasp, watch her fall into the sea below. This time her eyes had seemed different, yes, darker, deeper, without the fear, for they had become the eyes of Mary Jayne.

His head, damn it, it was starting again. The old familiar pain that was his to bear since his boyhood. *Hush little baby don't say a word, mamma's gonna buy you a mocking bird.* The gentle rhythm floated hauntingly round the house. Bella awoke with a chill to her spine. He was back, the party was over.

It has been some time since Mary Jayne had put on her business suit and played the part of a professional woman. She liked the feel of it, it felt good. Though on second thoughts, maybe the suit was a little too much? After all, the meeting would be a mixed group of mums from all areas of Liverpool. What the hell! She liked the way the pencil skirt showed her figure. Was there anything wrong with looking womanly, mother or not?

So, maybe she was joining the campaign just as a means to get her out of the house for a couple of hours a week. Was that so bad? Besides, she did believe in the general ideas of the 'Mother Community Forum'.

The Town Hall stood strong and looming in the centre of Liverpool, its two vast pillars announcing its importance to the world. They were fortunate indeed at having been given the use of a free meeting room as and when they needed it.

William Liptrot, Leader of the Council, greeted Blake with a welcome fit for a visiting dignitary. Such was his fear of this man.

'Let's go to my private quarters, we can talk over a scotch. Conran, I can assure you it's the best.'

Conran accepted but he was already bored, his eyes offended by the vision of the fat and immensely ugly little man. Liptrot had that smell about him, the smell of old flesh, one might say.

Running fifteen minutes late for the very first meeting, Mary Jayne dashed round the corridors of the Town Hall like a woman possessed. So much for the in-control, image she thought, as a black curl swung loose from the bun at the back of her head.

It was an accident waiting to happen - her high-heeled black shoes and the recently polished marble flooring. A head-on collision. It was inevitable.

Andrew Simpson tucked into a cheese and pickle on brown whilst inspecting the carnage of an R.T.A. The bloodied and mangled bodies of two young boys aged no more than sixteen still lay sprawled across the interior of the car.

'Shit!' Simpson bawled, causing the young PC at his side to almost jump out of his boots. 'I said no fucking onions!'

'Sir!' shouted a nervous PC, new to the job.

'What is it?'

The PC handed Simpson a sheet of paper found on the floor of the car. Written on it were dates and times, not to mention a large sum of money marked clearly beside an address. Alongside the two shopping bags containing cocaine, it was pretty simple to understand.

Andrew was a happy man and even raised a smile of congratulation for himself.

'Sir!' shouted the PC again. 'Sir, pardon me, it's just that, well, you said for me to inform the parents and well...'

'Well?'

'Well, it's my first time. I feel a bit... nervous.'

'Don't worry, they'll be over it by opening time.' With that Simpson sniggered and left the rookie cop in disbelief.

It was impossible to attend the meeting. She couldn't, it was unthinkable. She'd give her apologies at the next meeting. Yes. That was the thing to do. My God, it was him. He looked shocked. She looked shocked. His eyes bored into her. His sincere apologies turned to shock upon recognition.

Slightly bruised and shaky, Mary Jayne parked the car, just missing David's bike, which had been carelessly left in the drive over night. Running into the house and up the stairs, she threw herself on top of the bed. He was in her head once again. It was like he had never left, his face was so clear. He was what she craved. One night of passion. Just one night and the world would turn a blind eye. Closing her eyes, she lingered at the memory of him before her, the memory of his gaze, arrogant and intimate, yet delightful. The tall, lean body, the thick well-groomed hair; how commanding he had looked in his black shirt and black trousers. His skin was olive and smooth. Would his age bring gifts and the magic of experience to his hands?

Now, just for moments, her fingers became his as her knees parted and she allowed her hand to travel. Almost with ceremony, his fingers reached inside her plain black pants to touch her flesh, his fingers so sure and firm on her skin. Gasping for more, her body submitted and yielded to his touch. He became her inquisitor as he toyed with her, controlling each orgasm. It was for his touch to allow how and when. He laughed at her as he mastered her clitoris, for she was now his, and oh, the joy he felt! Now abrupt, he spread her legs, pulled down her underwear, licked and teased her. Using his tongue to taste, he enjoyed her. Growing weak, she became a structure of orgasms and flowing juices until she felt the force of his hands as he turned her over. Whilst stimulating her clitoris, he gently introduced his finger into the beginnings of her anal passage. Mary Jayne was shocked at the perversity of it. Horrified, she wanted more.

Conran had left Liptrot, promising to have a girl available for fun right after Friday's council bash. Someone who needed to be introduced to pleasure would be most suitable for Liptrot and the boys. Yes, a dirty girl would be grand. He would have agreed to supply the entire Convent of St Mary's if it meant he could get away as soon as possible. For she had found him - or perhaps he had found her. No matter, it was a sign. He would have beauty in his life again. It was time. He must cleanse himself of all sin, purge his soul of the past.

CHAPTER 21

Operation Merlin was set up and organised with in hours. It was of course all thanks to the little sheet of paper found in the previous R.T.A. Without a shadow of a doubt, the information on that paper would lead to another major drugs bust. Andrew Simpson visualised himself in the position of Commander.

Thanking Barnsey for breaking his leave at short notice and promptly coming down to the station, Simpson fully informed his partner and provided all the details of operation Merlin. Barnsey was horrified when told the details. My God, that was Blake's drop and only yesterday, Barnsey had given them the all clear to go ahead.

'Is there something bothering you, Barnsey, old friend. Thought you'd be glad of the action?' mouthed Simpson.

'No, no. Just come as a surprise that's all. You know, gotta get psyched up and all that'.

He had to get to a phone, had to get word to Blake, and he had to do it within the next ten minutes.

Bella sat back and lit another fag whilst at the same time shovelling chocolate liqueurs into her scabby mouth. Gulping down Conran's best brandy, she swung round on the desk chair like a child playing office. Feeling grand, she wanted to play at being boss.

'You start sucking up my ass now or its curtains, you cunt,' she giggled, enthralled at her play. Spreading her legs on top of the desk, she got quite carried away. 'Bella coffee. Bella you useless bitch, coffee now, Bella, Bella, Bella!'

She had often wondered what it felt like to be Conran Blake, the feared and powerful Conran Blake. Yes, she liked the feel of it indeed. Pouring more bandy and dragging on her fag, she was about to continue her performance when the ringing of the telephone startled her.

'Shit!' She dropped her fag, scrambled to get it whilst holding the telephone.

'Blake, it's me,' a voice whispered urgently. 'You have to stop the drop. Can you hear me? Stop it now. Clear everything out fast. Clean the place not a trace must be left. Can't talk now.' The line went dead.

Bella knew the voice was Barnsey's. Hell! She had to contact Conran, but where? Country Club having lunch. No, no, playing golf. Yes he must be playing golf. Scrambling through the pages of the phone book, she suddenly stopped.

'Why am I doing this?' she reflected. Slowly, she put the book down, gulped her brandy and sat back, grinning.

The casino was shut to everyone except Blake and his mistress Wendy. In a dark, dank cellar a heavily proportioned woman ordered the grown boy in front of her to remove his trousers. Desiring yet fearing the sting of the leather strap, Blake obeyed.

'Pants, remove them, I need to see if you have been sinning again.' Forcing the body to bend and touch his toes, she applied the lubricant around his anus. The boy man moaned with fear and pleasure.

'You have been touching yourself, haven't you? What disgusting thing have we been doing? Have we been playing with our pencil? Did you touch it like this?'

Reaching between his legs, her plump hands took hold of his well-formed and erect cock.

'What shall Mummy do with a dirty boy, a sinner?'

The familiar sting and heat of the strap told him he was home again, once more in the control of his mother. No longer would he need to think and work things out. He was the little boy again, so very loved and cossetted by his strict mother. The dark was comfort to him and the smell of darkness was as it always had been when he was a child. It was safe now to be small. Soon he would be cleansed of his sin and God would send love to him again.

Tony Griffin took his seat on the plane, knowing this would be his last trip as a free man. Today, he thought, should have been dull and overcast. Yet the clear blue sky seemed to mock his plight. Never again would he feel the warmth of the Spanish sun on his back or bathe in the crystal clear ocean. From now on, a simple stroll along the commercialised Costa del Sol sea front would be the stuff of dreams. For Tony Griffin, a long and harsh sentence served at Her Majesty's pleasure awaited him. First, he would spend brief moments reunited with his beloved wife, holding her close to him, smelling her perfume, touching her tender cheek before they took him away. Just one kiss from his daughter would have to see him through the dark days of his incarceration. In many years to come he would be a free man, having paid for his life of crime. Tony Griffin would walk the streets without fear of reprisals, for surely by that time the Blake Empire would have long since crumbled. Yes, Tony Griffin was ready to tell all in return for a lighter sentence and a future in England with his family.

Blake didn't bother to sign in, much to the annoyance of the Town Hall receptionist. He knew he would not be staying long. Today she would come once again to attend the 'Mothers' Forum '. His detective work had paid off. Now all he had to do was wait. This second meeting would not be by chance.

He scanned the brochures scattered on the reception table ready for waiting guests. Now and again he would look up to view everyone who entered and signed in: councillors, business people, council administrators, all of no interest to Blake - until finally his raven-haired beauty stood before him.

She had known he would be waiting. Her heart and her conscience were prepared to do what she could not resist.

Without speaking, the two strangers, both charged with sexual energy and anticipating the joy to come, drove quietly to the house of Conran Blake.

Andrew Simpson was still basking in the glory of his recent triumph. His lust for success grew stronger and his ambition to succeed ran like a rampant virus through his veins. Ideas formed in his head, images of the future kept his hunger alive as he vowed to clear the streets of all crime. On a one-man crusade, Andrew Simpson worked night and day.

Turning the audiotape off, he leaned forward, getting as close as possible to the face of Tony Griffin. Whispering, he promised a deal in return for information. Chief Inspector Simpson wanted to know everything, right from the beginning.

It was hard for Tony to recall the early years spent on Conran Blake's payroll. He had been just a lad back then on the streets of Skimsdale. Finding employment that paid well had been hard, he remembered, and his intention had only ever been to make a couple of quid to help set up his own business. Do a couple of deals, run the risk for a week or two, just to sort himself out. He could not have known Blake would blackmail him and threaten him. That his life would no longer be his own.

Simpson, though shocked, made a successful attempt to hide his feelings. To let this low-life know they were both from the same background and town would have been belittling. After all, this man before him was scum, and the thought of any possible comparison to himself would be too much to bear. Besides, Andrew Simpson had kept his cheap and nasty childhood to himself. He was not proud of it and felt he deserved something better and more up-market. As far as most people knew, he was the product of a good family, well thought of in the Shevington area.

Griffin stuttered in his recollection of the once faded memories that now came back bold as brass as if they had simply been placed on file for this very occasion. Maybe they had been.

'I was about to tell Blake I'd had enough, wanted out, didn't want to run any more deals, no more drugs. I wasn't suited you see, I…'

'Go on slowly. No rush. Take your time,' Simpson urged him gently.

'I can see it so clear, oh God! oh God! I can smell the blood. Oh, sweet Jesus! The smell. Her hair was matted; she was young, so young! Both dead! His body. I couldn't get his body into the bag, my hands were covered in blood, they kept slipping. Damn, Jesus help me! He wouldn't fit into the bag!' Tony cried as if it had been only yesterday.

'Who did you kill, Tony?'

Now really agitated, Tony shouted, 'No No! Didn't kill anyone. Was sent by the devil to clean up the mess.'

'Who did they kill, Tony?'

'He was my best friend you see, Johnny Simpson was my friend.'

Aghast with horror, Andrew felt as if the blood in his veins had turned cold. He felt sick. His head began to spin. Must get out, get away from this man. In the men's cloakroom the Chief Inspector vomited and coughed until his body could take no more.

All these years he had managed to block out the memory of the little brother he had loved, the brother who had been murdered. Now the memory of his past consumed him and once again he returned to the dirt and squalor that was his youth, the hovel they called home, his dirty, dirty slag of a mother sitting dragging on a fag and swearing at him. Johnny, cheerful and full of love, saying not to worry about things. Yea, Johnny always said he worried too much. Kind-hearted Johnny; happy-go-lucky Johnny. Dead Johnny.

Andrew Simpson for the first time in twenty years felt the coldness of wet salty tears fall upon his face. Only then did he draw the file on Conran Blake, the file that told everything he didn't want to know.

Mary Jayne could feel no guilt and that scared her. Surely she should feel something other then alive and excited. Her mood was dark, not angry or rebellious but quietly reserved as she was coming to terms with who she really was. In this small but beautifully furnished bedroom, coloured in rich terracotta and orange, Mary Jayne had changed her life perhaps forever. No longer could she hide behind the screen of mother and respectable wife; that was not for her, she was no longer any of those things. Her fate she did not know and no matter how scared she was, she enjoyed not knowing. It excited her.

Now she would have to learn to live two lives until the time came when she could cast off her robes of motherhood and begin again. What of the love she had proclaimed for her husband? She didn't know. Stability, it seemed, had been her only desire then.

Conran looked into the future and that of his empire. He would need to start cleaning up his act. From now on security would be tighter, discipline harsher and recruitment stricter. He would gain respect from all and rule as a true leader should. One day he would once again have a beauty by his side, a beauty he would possess and own but above all love. Yes, he would love her as he had never loved before. This time he would be worthy.

In the dead of night Barnsey turned his engine off and sat in wait. The car park was empty of all life and noise. The sheer silence made him feel creepy. Just two miles away, in the town centre, people would be about the streets, going to the theatre, visiting restaurants, clubs and casinos. How he wished on this night he was with them.

Pulling his big winter coat tightly around his shoulders, he glanced up and saw a figure emerge from the darkness. It was tall and lean, he could see that, and the way the open trench coat flapped in the movement of the walk made Conran Blake look awesome and powerful as he strolled at a leisurely pace towards the car.

Barnsey knew he would have to convince Blake that he had

indeed tried to tip him off. He had made the phone call in time, he had done his job. It was no fault of his that the bust had gone ahead. But how to prove himself, he had no idea.

Conran took his position in the passenger seat as Barnsey babbled on and on. Turning to look the little fat copper in the face, Conran gave a gentle smile and suggested they take in the evening air. As they walked, Blake began to hum a lullaby. Barnsey thought it was weird. In fact, it scared the shit out of him.

'Hush little baby don't say a word, pappa's gonna buy you a mocking bird.'

From the shadows stalked Gregory Scott and another of Conran's henchmen. To some, the whimpering cries of the fat, balding man would have aroused pity, but their eyes were steely as they removed his trousers. Barnsey fought, but fear rendered him almost useless. Scott smirked to himself. Sometime to-morrow, someone would find a corpse lying on the side of the road with a penis sticking out of its mouth. God, how funny would that be?

She didn't pull the sheet to cover her nakedness as she once would have immediately after sex. Now she lay naked and exposed, comfortable. Bathing in the afterglow, she closed her eyes and slept for a short while, her desire fulfilled..

Sleep begged him to pay heed, yet he fought to stay awake. Every moment counted, every minute she lay beside him was precious. Her hunger for him had perhaps shocked and pleased him; it had been so long since he had felt wanted and desired, truly desired. Her body had willingly moved to his touch, open to suggestion and pleasure. Every movement had been sensu-ous and easy, not awkward or clumsy.

Today Conran Blake had reason to look to the future.

CHAPTER 22

Andrew Simpson read the file on Blake. It made interesting reading, documenting crimes in which Blake was suspected of involvement, but for which there was no concrete evidence, so no prosecution had ever been possible. When he got to page 107, Andrew's attention turned to horror and disbelief. It was not possible, could not be. Achill Island; the name Morgan Blake; accidental death by drowning. According to the coroner's report, there was no evidence to link Mr Blake with the death of Mrs Blake. Also documented in brackets, was Mrs Blake's maiden name: Lahiffe.

Andrew froze as the horror unfolded. He read again the names, Lahiffe, Morgan Lahiffe, Morgan Blake, Lahiffe, Ireland, Achill Island. There could be no mistake and no coincidence. Andrew Simpson, Chief Inspector of the CID, had been tricked into marrying the daughter of a whore, fathered by a killer. Indeed he had married someone no better than his own mother. The feelings of shame and disgrace he had felt as a child became once again real as he revisited the past, recognising the pungent smell of stale beer and cheap vodka.

The voice of his drunken mother rang loud in his head.

'Fuck off, you little cunt. Get to bed or I'll wipe the floor with you. Me and lover boy here have things to do. Right that in't it, Uncle? Oh fuck it, who cares anyway, eh! You bastard save some for me. Just a little old drop to get old Deloris in the mood to give you a good seeing to or you can suck your own dick. Wait, get your paws off, let me take mi tights off, mi gusset's lathered.'

The telephone rang, ending the vision. He didn't answer it, fearing it was his mother... no, he meant his wife. That clever,

143

educated lady, well bred, brought up amongst the good folk of Achill Island where no sin was tolerated and no crime rate possible. Tricked. He had been deceived, he was a man wronged. His wife was no better than a dirty cheap whore, fathered by scum.

The water trickled over her face and down her body as she closed her eyes to enjoy the soothing sensation of the hot flow. How good it felt to be fulfilled. Would it always be like this? Was this satisfaction? She hoped so. Putting her head back, she closed her eyes and dreamt of the next time she would touch him.

The bathroom door did not bang but closed quietly. He stood watching her, the woman in the mist. Such beauty crafted to perfection, the shoulders, the firm breasts, the contours of her body a delight to look upon. How could it be so, how was it possible for the daughter of a whore and a killer to be so blessed in beauty? There should have been a mark, a blemish, a sign of sin. After all, one only had to look at his mother to see what she was and what stock she was born of: scum, low-life common scum.

Her heart skipped as she stepped from the shower to find him there glaring in a trance- like state.

'Darling, I didn't hear you come in. You're early. Is everything all right?'

He gave no response. She felt vulnerable standing naked before him. With her arms, she covered her breasts and asked for the robe that hung from the door.

'Andrew, why are you staring at me? Are you ill?'

As she reached for the towel rail his hand shot out to stop her. She jumped back.

'Jesus Christ, Andrew! What's wrong with you? I need a towel, I'm getting cold'.

Still holding her wrist with his other hand, he grabbed the back of her neck, his grip tight enough to force her to look into the mirror.

144

'Stop it. Let me go', she cried. 'Why are you doing this to me?'

Mocking him. She was mocking him just like his mother had mocked him. This time he could stop her. This time he would stop her. He felt a surge of power as he rammed his wife's face into the mirror. He lost his grip as her body fell forwards over the sink. He gripped again and held the face once again in front of the fragmented glass.

How was it possible? How could it be that with such lacerations and the face seeping blood she still looked beautiful and wholesome, still no hint of the scum she really was? Her body was limp and lifeless as he picked her up and placed her in the bath. The cold running water roused her to a dazed state. The bath was almost full. The water turned a gentle shade of pink as the blood from her wounds ran down her face. Freezing now, she lay in the bath and for the life of her she had not the strength to get out. Then an aroma rose to her nostrils, strong and pungent, familiar. He was pouring something into the water. With terror in her heart, she passed out.

Andrew Simpson emptied the last drop of bleach into the bath. Taking a sponge, he knelt down and began to wash the sin from his wife. Opening her legs, he inserted the last drop of bleach. Soon she would be clean, clean enough to meet her Father and her Maker.

CHAPTER 23

Conran Blake stared at the pile of paperwork before him. It was no use. He had no interest today, or motivation. A woman was on his mind. A beautiful-dark haired woman, a woman he could love till the end of his days. Was this truly his second chance? After all, the past had done him wrong. He had been deceived by the cruel hand of fate. Perhaps she was a gift. Why not? He deserved her, didn't he? He deserved to be loved, especially after the last time. No, no, he would not go there. He would not think about the woman who had hurt him badly, it was all in the past. Today he was happy, and what's more, his head was clear, there would be no pain.

This time he vowed to love and cherish her, give her everything, protect her from the world if need be. Perhaps there would even be a child - she was still young enough. There would be holidays, Christmas and good times. Conran Blake smiled. He was happy, truly happy.

Bella slammed the tray on the desk, almost spilling the coffee onto the papers. 'Anything else?' she snarled.

He laughed. Today she was funny. He had never found her funny before but today he could not help but laugh at her.

'Bella, Bella,' he said smiling.

'What the fuck's up with you?'

How ugly she was, he thought. The years of drug abuse had made her so. The poxy, spotty face, the scabby thin lips. My God she was a sight. Under the scrutiny of his gaze, she suddenly felt awkward and uncomfortable.

'Oh, Bella. How long have we known each other now? Many years and you know, I've never really realised quite how ugly you are. You're not a real woman, are you, Bella? What are you? Don't you long to be beautiful? No, I expect not. What would you do without me, Bella? No man would want you. No, its not for you, is it Bella?'

Out of the top drawer he took a large bag of cocaine. 'Here, take this. A little extra for you to enjoy. Go on take your lover away with you and do your thing. Poor Bella!' Yes. She was amusing today. She made him laugh.

Grabbing the bag, she left the library and ran to the comfort of her own room. Sitting on the edge of the bed she opened the bag and dipped her stained and dirty finger into it as deep as she could. Putting the finger to her mouth, she sucked off the powder with the insistence of a child suckling at its mother's breast.

Bella cried for the first time in years. She sobbed and sobbed, something she had thought she would never do again in her lifetime. It had been so long since she'd felt any emotion, be it hurt, sadness, or even happiness. He had never called her ugly before. In fact he had never paid her any personal attention for the past ten years. She had simply been the one to clean his house, cook his meals, wash his pants, take the abuse. Today he had hurt her badly, for she loved Conran Blake, had loved him all these years. Deep down, somewhere inside, she had hoped for the impossible: his love. How ludicrous it was, how completely impossible and insane, the very idea that he could ever love her.

Sitting alone on her bed Bella cried.

Slowly she gained consciousness. Water. There had been water, cold so very cold, then the pain. Her face hurt badly. Someone had dressed her, she could remember feeling hands on her body. Where was she? Hands, she was being lifted. A car. She was being lifted out of a vehicle.

It was dark as he carried the injured creature out of the car and across the street to the front door of Conran Blake's house.

Jesus, what was that banging! Conran rushed to the front door swearing to do harm to Scott for making so much noise.

He opened the door. Simpson rushed in, dragging alongside him the weak and limp body of his wife.

It took moments for Conran to recognise his love as he picked her up and carried her to the library. Simpson watched. Yes, perhaps he knew she was his daughter, perhaps he knew already. It was possible. After all, he seemed familiar with her.

'What have you done to her?' cried Blake as he stared into the lacerated face.

'May I introduce myself and my darling wife.' Simpson then pulled a gun from his pocket.

It made sense now to Blake. He must have found out somehow. Perhaps she had decided to tell him so that they could be together sooner. Oh! Why hadn't she waited till they could tell him together? He could have protected her from this animal, this monster. Kneeling down, he took her head in his hands and kissed her through his tears.

'You've know all along, haven't you?' said Simpson. 'No wonder you would have nothing to do with the whore. I'll bet you've enjoyed watching from a distance, haven't you? Tell me, when were you going to claim her? When were you going to choose the moment to ruin my career and reputation by claiming this whore as your daughter? Was it not enough to kill my brother all those years ago? What did Johnny do to you to make you murder him so ruthlessly?'

Blake held still. This man was mad, obviously mad.

'What are y...'

Pulling out the papers he had removed from Blake's file, Andrew threw them on the floor. The first was a news clipping telling of the death of Johnny Simpson, the second a picture of Morgan and the text relating all the details of her death on Achill Island

Blake read the first but had no recollection of the boy. The second he read and still did not understand as for the first time he looked into the face of Andrew Simpson.

'Don't you see a resemblance? Yes, she has a look of her dead mother, don't you think? There, I've brought the father his long-lost daughter. Aren't you going to thank me, both of you?' he shouted.

Blake turned the colour of a corpse as he read the police report relaying the details of his wife's tragic fall from the cliff.

'Now take a good look at this pretty little picture, one of my wife's most treasured possessions.'

Blake stared at the picture of a young Morgan standing beside a sign that read 'Welcome To Achill Island'. The inscription on the back read: 'Morgan Aged 16', then underneath: 'To Mary Jayne on your 16th birthday, your mother would have been proud. Love Uncle Robert.'

The soul of Conran Blake cried out.

Mary Jayne finally opened her eyes to see before her the tortured face of her lover

'Please, Conran, stop him. He'll kill us both'.

'Ah!' cried Simpson with a strange and almost humorous tone in his voice. 'So my darling wife does know her father. How sweet of her never to introduce me. I can't think why!'

'Father, father? He's not my father, Andrew, he's my lover'

Simpson turned his back upon the scene as the vomit reached his throat.

The door opened suddenly. Bella entered, raised the gun she held in her right hand and shot three bullets into the head of Andrew Simpson.

'I was lying down. I could hear shouting and noises,' she said, still pointing the gun.

'Give me the gun, Bella,' Conran commanded.

'What, oh this, oh yea.'

Looking down, she stared at the woman on the floor. Despite the dreadful facial wounds, Bella could see that she was very pretty, beautiful in fact. How she envied her .

Blake reached for the gun. Bella recognised her moment of absolute power and stepped back out of his reach.

'No, no, don't force me, Conran, stay still. Stay where you are. I want to look at her some more. I want to just look at her.'

Mary Jayne paid no attention to the woman with the gun for

all she cared about now was the truth. Her voice low and gentle, she said. 'Is it true, please tell me, is it true? Are you my father?'

'Go on, Blake, tell her the truth. Go on, let's see if she can handle what a fuck-up she really is, even if she is a beautiful fuck up!'

'What is she talking about, please?' Mary Jayne cried. 'Please, someone has to tell me what's going on'.

Blake took hold of the clippings, the pictures and the police report . Now as gentle as any man could be, he laid them before her.

'It's true about your mother. She was my wife. I loved her very much. But she betrayed me. But it's okay, we can still be together. You're not my child, I promise you, Mary Jayne. You're not my daughter. Your mother, she had someone else. You're not my child.' His voice begged for the future. 'Please, we can still be together. We can make it work'.

Bella laughed, now she had him big time. As she opened her mouth to speak, he turned on her, his voice threatening.

'Be quiet Bella. I warn you. Shut your ugly mouth or God help me I'll tear you apart.'

'Well fuck me, Conran! You're something fucking else,' she said. This was unbelievable. He still had the audacity to push her around, even with a forty-four calibre pointing at him.

As Mary Jayne managed to struggle to her feet, the gun was pointed in her direction.

'And just where the fuck do you think you're off to? It's not over yet, is it, Conran? Oh no, the show has only just begun.'

'I love you, Mary Jayne, oh God I love you, don't you see that, we can still be together. For God's sake, tell me you still want me, tell me!'

'It's over. It's different now. How can we ever be happy? Perhaps in time…'

No, no, not even in time, thought Bella. She would have to know the truth. Let's see if she still loved him when she knew just what Conran Blake was capable of. After all, if she were condemned to a life of misery, then this time he would share it with her.

'You'd better tell her the truth, Conran, or I'll blow a fucking hole in your head the size of a football pitch.'

'No. Shoot. Go on bitch, shoot! What does it matter now? I'd rather be dead than live without Mary Jayne. I swear, I'd rather be dead. Go on Bella do it. Ah! but then, who would take care of you? How would you live without your regular supply? Just think about it, Bella.'

It was no longer the coke that mattered. Her heart was breaking and the world had nothing to offer her, so why stick around? Bella was prepared for the worst, even if it was to be done by her own hand. No, the supply of drugs would not be needed.

'Though I hate to have to tell you this, sweetheart, mummy didn't fall off that cliff, did she Conran?'

'Bella,' he screamed, 'for God sake!'

'Oh Conran, you look really ugly when you shout like that. Have I ever told you that before, ha?' Oh it felt good this, felt real good. Bella was starting to enjoy herself.

'What do you mean?' pleaded Mary Jayne. 'She fell. Please tell me she fell. My mother fell.' What was this woman trying to do to her and why? She knew nothing of this woman with the gun.

'He pushed her off the Cliff. He killed your mother. How does it feel to have been shagging your mother's murderer?'

Fuelled with hatred, all sense was gone as Mary Jayne rushed towards Bella, took hold of the gun, held it in Bella's direction and pulled the trigger. But the bullet clipped her side, causing only a superficial wound.

'Look for yourself. I'm not lying to you, why should I? If you kill me how will you ever know the truth? Your father's name was Justin. They found his body but Mr Blake here was too good, too clever. They never pinned it on him. Trust me, you stupid bitch, it's true.'.

Mary Jayne reached out and grabbed all the papers and clippings. It was true, all true. Here in black and white, her mother's name, where she came from, the name of Achill. Oh God. It was all true. The man she had shared a bed with, the man she had allowed to touch her intimately and lovingly, the man she had enjoyed, had killed her precious mother.

For him, death would have been too kind.

CHAPTER 24

The morning was bright as the sun shot through the windows. Opening the curtains and gazing out at a bright blue sky, Bella could not remember. Had there ever been a day so bright as this one? Still, no time to dilly-dally. It was a school day and time to get the children out of bed, always a task in itself as David and Catherine loved to sleep late. First the school run and, if she remembered correctly, Mary Jayne had ordered the car to be fuelled and ready to pay a visit. It was good being able to remember things. She liked it, in fact she liked everything about her life these days, not least of all the way her skin glowed and her eyes shone. Yes, coming off the coke and meeting the boss was the best thing that had ever happened to her.

Mary Jayne pondered on the many things she had to do, the many meeting she had to attend. Thank goodness for Bella. That girl was worth her weight in gold. It was all very well running one casino, that would have been easy, but four... Oh well. Business was good and that was all she cared about.

As ever, the nursing staff showed great care and dedication at all times. Money was a marvellous thing, for there had been a long waiting list for accommodation at Sleepy Pastures Nursing Home, it was so well respected.

Oh yes, money was indeed a marvellous thing. It had also helped with the expensive skin treatments that made her burns barely noticeable now.

The girl behind the desk could not help but admire the woman who signed the guest book. She was classy and very attractive in her designer suits and tall black boots, the gloves made out of fine leather. Ah, to be that beautiful and that rich, one could only dream. Still, this poor woman had her lot to bear. She was dedicated to her old and infirm father, poor paralysed soul that he was. No, she never missed a visit, regular as clockwork every week, always taking time to spoon-feed him his favourite treat. She was a good daughter. He had every reason to be proud.

In a small room that had the pleasure of overlooking the grounds, a man sat alone. His eyes could just see the sunlight and if someone moved his wheelchair he would be able to see the trees. That would be nice. The tongue started to protrude from the mouth. Damn it, proclaimed the voice in his head, for he could not reach the straw that would enable him to take a drink. Where was that lazy fucking nurse? he thought, as the piss started to run down his useless legs.

It was too late. The man's angry eyes moved from side to side with frustration as he realised that he needed to be toiletted again.